COMPTON CHICK

COMPTON CHICK

Alex Tyson

URBAN BOOKS
www.urbanbooks.net

Urban Books
10 Brennan Place
Deer Park, NY 11729

ISBN-13: 978-1-893196-77-3
ISBN-10: 1-893196-77-1

First Printing February 2007
Printed in the United States of America

10   9   8   7   6   5   4   3   2   1

*This is a work of fiction. Any references or similarities to actual events, real
people, living, or dead, or to real locales are intended to give the novel a
sense of reality. Any similarity in other names, characters, places, and inci-
dents is entirely coincidental.*

Submit Wholesale Orders to:
Kensington Publishing Corp.
C/O Penguin Group (USA) Inc.
Attention: Order Processing
405 Murray Hill Parkway
East Rutherford, NJ 07073-2316
Phone: 1-800-526-0275
Fax: 1-800-227-9604

Part I

Chapter 1

Compton, California

July 4, 1983 was a day Jackie would always remember, not so much because it was a holiday, but because she would always recall it years later as a watershed that marked the end of her girlhood.

The neighbors and friends had gathered to celebrate America's Independence Day in the communal yard outside their apartment, which was bare of grass. The hickory smells of barbecue ribs, chicken, and hot dogs eddied and swirled around the back patio, sending mouth-watering signals throughout the projects.

Few seemed bothered by the fact that the Revolutionary War fought three hundred years earlier had not been with their collective freedom in mind. The way everyone moved with graceful abandon, one would have thought they were free, instead of existing in the confines of the Abraham Lincoln's Projects in Compton, California. Many were dancing barefoot on the cement. The residents called it *nigger grass.*

Public housing, better known as the projects, had begun in the United States in the 1950s. The Lincoln Project had been conceived in the '50s too. In its original conception, it was meant to be a step-up for low-income families, but in the ensuing years, it became a prison to many who lived within its confines, and a blight on the flourishing Hollywood Beverly Hills community.

Peopled by young and old unemployed men and women, the denizens had plenty of time on their hands, if not enough money, and spent their days sitting on stoops and holding up the street corners.

Stooped against a leaden sky, the anemic-looking buildings resembled army barracks, the fronds of the few palm trees, which hadn't been cut down, swaying back and forth in the gentle wind.

Although only a few sunrays pierced the smog, everyone was relieved that it hadn't rained. Bright smiles colored the rainbow of cashew-, almond-, and coconut shell-hued faces.

Away from the crowd, Jackie plopped down on a milk crate at the end of the yard. She had never felt so anti-social or more depressed in her sixteen years. Absent-mindedly, she chewed on her fingernails as she secretly examined her family. She felt like a ghost staring down at the holiday revelry. It was as if she was seeing everything through a different pair of eyes. Twisting her "dookie" braid that had slipped from her crown, she sighed.

Generally, she enjoyed just admiring her four sisters and one brother, who all ranged in color from butterscotch to vanilla cream to mocha fudge, yet, in a different way, all resembled both of her parents. They all had the same high foreheads, the same cat eyes, as they called them in the projects, and the same full noses, the only difference being, two of her sisters had hazel eyes and one had grayish-blue eyes. Jackie's eyes were a light amber color, sometimes making her look like a tigress hidden in the trees and about to strike.

Even her parents had striking looks, which made people turn around and take a second look at them. Her mother, a smooth chamois brown complexion, still possessed a youthful figure. People often said she looked like a dark-skinned Dorothy Dandridge. Her father, a Creole, was a dead ringer for a light-skinned Clark Gable.

Jackie had always considered herself blessed to have such a unique-looking family, but today was different. Nothing or no one felt right anymore.

Usually, on the various summer holidays, she was comforted by the familiar smells of pig feet, barbecue ribs, and hot dogs as they spit their juices on the coals below the grill, not to mention that corn on the cob, collard greens, pork 'n' beans, hot dog buns, and potato salad had always provided her with a sense of safety and security, representing home.

Everyone said that Wu Tsing, the local butcher, made a killing as most of the families in the projects tended to overbuy on the holidays. His wife Suyuann had stood behind the counter, a bright smile plastered on her face, as she spoke part Chinese and part Ebonics. "Hey, Mama, pig feet and chicken feet on sale. You like?"

Jackie remembered her father complaining bitterly about foreigners coming to the neighborhood and black people spending money with them and not with him at his corner store.

"This is crazy," he'd say. "What is wrong with our people?"

Didn't matter that the next day, money would be short, and someone's child, dressed to kill the day before in a new rainbow-brilliant outfit and a pair of the latest expensive brand-name tennis shoes, would have to knock on a neighbor's door and say, "Miss Ernestine, my mama say could she borrow a cup of sugar?"

"Okay, don't forget to bring back the bowl. It's part of a set the kids gave me for Mother's Day, and I don't want to lose it. By the way, I think your mother has another bowl from me from last week."

Nobody was thinking about the other 364 days in the year, just as long as they could go all out on the upcoming holiday. In fact it didn't even have to be a holiday. Whether it was just a weekend on which the weather was fine or there was a party in the neighborhood, it seemed everyone had to be sporting the latest. In fact there was a fashion parade going on all the time, and nobody wanted to be outdone.

Mr. Smalls had become more and more despondent over the situation and, from what Jackie gathered from his late-night conversations with her mother, had sold his mom-and-pop store after ten years of trying to eke out a living.

* * *

With Prince screaming "When Doves Cry," in the background, and the crowd swaying back and forth, the air quivered with a happiness that only the residents understood. For now, no one was worried about the fact that they had an overdue light bill, that they didn't have a bank account, savings or checking, that cousin Pookie was in jail, or that Jabari's fourteen-year-old niece, Shoshana, was accidentally shot in a drive-by.

Today, for once, there was peace. The Bloods and the Crips even seemed to be laying low. The crackling of gunfire, the buzzing of helicopters overhead, the screaming of police sirens in the near distance hadn't soured the day. Only regular firecrackers and cherry bombs pierced the hazy day.

Outside Jackie's backyard, one could even hear a group of little girls playing double dutch, jumping rope to a rhythmic thump. Obviously, their mothers felt it was safe for them to play on the sidewalks that day.

The girls sang, "Rock steady, 'cause your team ain't ready."

Bopping their heads to the beat, the young, the old, and the not-so-young danced to a hidden rhythm which had traversed across the years and the continents.

Jackie glanced over at her father's friends, Wild Bill, Cowboy, and King, as they slapped dominoes on a makeshift card table. Without missing a beat, they would pop open beer bottles and guzzle down the cool contents, Adam's apples moving up and down like oil rigs.

The younger neighborhood women—Nikki, Cabrille, Sheniqua, and Fox, to name a few—tight skirts hugging their curves and low-cut blouses revealing their cleavage, fanned their bosoms and flirted openly with the older women's husbands. Generally, in their early twenties and each of them having anywhere from two to four babies among them and no husbands, their lust-borne offspring were climbing all over the boxes, throwing toys, and playing in a mud pile.

Meantime, the older women, Miss Cleondra, Miss Ernestine, and Miss Johnnie Mae (the younger woman called them "tight-ass wives") rolled their eyes, but decided to indulge their husbands' waning egos.

All in all, everyone was having "a funky good time." Everyone wore white-hot smiles, except Jackie, but no one seemed to notice.

For the first time in her life, Jackie felt alienated from her sisters and brothers, to whom she'd always felt close. It was a source of silent pride for her that her parents lived together and that all six children had the same father, seldom the case in the projects. Hell, seldom the case in America, period.

A small commotion caught her attention.

Yolanda, Jackie's eleven-year-old sister, whom everyone called Yoyo from the time she could hold one, pleaded, "Ross, you and Cornbread do that dance, pretty pleaaasssee." She tugged on her brother's arm, as she dragged out the word *please.*

Yoyo's pale grayish eyes glittered when she looked from her 14-year-old brother to his friend, Cornbread, who was the same age. The two called themselves "play *brothers.*"

Everyone called Ross' friend, who was named Dennis at birth, "Cornbread," because he ate cornbread dipped in buttermilk all the time. His mother, Miss Johnnie Mae, had brought this tradition with her from the South.

Jackie could see Yoyo's sisterly affection for their only brother shining all over her face. She, too, was crazy about Ross. If he wasn't so level-headed, Ross could have been spoiled. All his sisters doted on him so, but Ross was a good son, a good brother, and a good student.

Ross flung his wet jheri curls back from his forehead, but held back his eagerness to display his dance talents and coolly declined. He threw up his hand in a hatchet-like symbol, a "Forget it," sign, to show how indifferent he was. He leaned against the wall, his baggy pants sagging comfortably, one leg rolled up, his double shoelaces untied, and chewed on a toothpick lodged in the corner of his mouth. "Nah!"

Cornbread, who idolized him, looked to Ross for the sign to relent and decided to act nonchalant also. In imitation of Ross, he threw up the edge of his hand. "Nah."

"Aw, pretty please," Lelani, the nine-year-old baby sister enjoined, jumping from one foot to the other.

"Yeah, go on and dance," Annette said. At seventeen, she was the eldest child and a take-charge kind of girl. When she spoke, the younger siblings listened. "We want to see this new breakdance."

Natasha, Jackie's thirteen-year-old sister, known as Tasha, started clapping and stomping her feet. "Yeah, go 'head."

The sisters, Tasha, Lelani, Yoyo, and Annette, formed a circle around Ross and Cornbread and chanted, "Go 'head! Go 'head! Go 'head!"

Yoyo suggested, "Let's put on 'Thriller,'" knowing that they all loved Michael Jackson's new album.

"Mom, can we change the record?"

Jackie watched as her mother, in charge of barbecuing, looked up from the round-bellied barrel, which served as a pit. Her eyes held a faraway look, like she had something on her mind. She nodded at Jackie.

The older couples who were slow dancing to B.B. King's, "The Thrill Is Gone," groaned in protest, as they pulled out of each other's arms.

Right away, Michael Jackson's voice and music blared out of the boom box and filled the yard.

Ross and Cornbread began an imitation of the "moon-walk," moving their shoulders in what was called the "popping and locking" moves, then began spinning on the ground, doing the breakdance.

Even the adults who'd stopped dancing circled the boys and clapped their hands and stomped their feet.

Night Train, the neighborhood wino, slurred, "Go, young bloods," between hiccups and sips from his brown-paper-bagged stash.

Tyrone, one of the older boys, called out, "Y'all should enter that street-dancing contest at the beach."

Jackie, who usually loved to dance and was known to be the best dancer in the family, didn't join in. Surreptitiously, she eyed the figures of her two teenaged sisters, Annette and Tasha. She'd never noticed before how flat their stomachs were. They both wore pedal pushers and fitted T-shirts. Even so, their modest looks screamed, "Nice girls."

How come I couldn't be more like them?

Jackie was the only one of her sisters who usually liked to knot her T-shirt up under her brassiere as soon as she stepped away from the house. She liked to roll her skirts up and wear the mini-look.

For the first time in her short life, she regretted how provocatively she had dressed since her breasts had sprouted and how she liked to look "fly." She was the only one of her adolescent sisters who liked to wear make-up, lipstick, and the big doorknocker earrings, something she'd done since the age of twelve. She'd also paint a sexy mole on her cheek, or wherever she had a pimple.

She didn't just wear dookie braids; she pulled them up in a crown so she could look older than her sixteen years.

Her spirit groaned inside. She thought to herself again, *How come I couldn't have been more like the other Smalls girls* (as they were known)? They always followed Mom's rules, including going to church and to Bible Study. But her . . . well . . . she had been sneaking around and living a double-life ever since her sophomore year of high school.

Someone put on Candi Staton's record, "Young Hearts Run Free."

As soon as the lyrics "Don't be no fool when love really don't love you" blasted into the yard, the words stabbed Jackie's heart.

Near the end of the song—"Encourage the babies when they say self-preservation is what's really going on"—Jackie had to bite her lip, to keep the tears from bursting out.

The song brought it all back to Jackie. She thought back to how she and Kenny met at the club a year ago.

After much pleading and cajoling, their mother had al-

11

lowed her and her sister, Annette, to go out, with the understanding that Annette was to watch Jackie.

"Annette, keep an eye on Jackie," had been Mrs. Smalls' exact words.

"Aw, Mom!" Jackie whined. She heaved a big sigh and rolled her eyes theatrically.

Looking back, it seemed as though, even a year ago, her mother had sensed that at fifteen, Jackie was a live cannon, waiting to be set off. Now, Jackie understood that her mother had known her better than she knew herself.

Suddenly Jackie felt such a strong urge to urinate, she was afraid she'd wet her pants. She jumped up from the crate, weaved her way through the dancers, and dashed into the house. She took the stairs, two at a time, to the second floor, where the bathroom was located at the end of the short hallway. Their unit, like all the others in the projects, was a two-story apartment. They had three bedrooms upstairs and considered themselves lucky, with there being five girls in the family. Ross was the only one with a makeshift bedroom.

When Jackie finished using the restroom, she found herself bent over the toilet bowel, where paroxysm after paroxysm attacked her young frame. She regurgitated all her entire breakfast. The slimy eggs and chips of bacon floated around the toilet and resembled a raw omelet. Face down in the toilet, hands on both sides of the bowl, she retched and retched, until she felt like she would pull her guts out if she didn't stop. Finally, after what seemed like an interminable time, the vomiting stopped.

In fact Jackie had been vomiting every day for the past few weeks and had learned to be as quiet as possible so that her sisters, who were usually in the other room, didn't hear her. Today, though, she was able to make a little more noise, since everyone was outside.

Jackie sat on the yellow linoleum floor with the golden-speckles circling around her. She felt emptied out. Sweat beads dotted her brow, and her top clung to her rib cage and felt clammy and damp.

Her mind tried to deny the truth, but her body wouldn't let her. What the nurse told her at the clinic was true. *"You're pregnant, young lady."*

That's why her breasts were so tender, and she constantly had to urinate. But she hadn't intended for things to go this far. How could she be pregnant? Wasn't she too young to have a baby? How could she have a baby, and she'd only started her period at fourteen and a half? What was she going to do? Her father was going to kill her.

Just thinking of her father's reaction to her pregnancy made a tremor run through her body. She'd always been the one he put on punishment the most, as she'd always been the most defiant.

Oh Lord!

Jackie splashed cold water on her face and stared at her reflection in the mirror. She looked the same. The same wet sandpaper-colored face, the same auburn hair twisted into thick dookie braids, the same slanted eyebrows and almond-shaped eyes that turned up at the corner.

Well, she did look a little sallow, but she was still the same old Jackie. What was she going to do?

While she bounded down the stairs, two at a time, everything seemed so strange. It was as though she was seeing the sepia-toned pictures of her grandparents, which were eye level on the staircase wall, through different eyes.

Her father's grandfather, Lance Smalls, was a white man. No wonder she and her brothers and sisters all had various shades of colors and funny-looking eyes. Jackie could swear his gray eyes were following her, as his serious mien looked down from the mahogany frame.

As Jackie slid down the worn brown carpet, a habit she began as a little girl, a thought occurred to her. She pondered throwing herself down the stairs. She'd once read that if a woman fell down a flight of stairs while pregnant, she would lose her baby.

Then she changed her mind. She was too afraid. *Nah! With my luck, I would break my neck and still be pregnant.*

When she landed in the midst of the living room, she took in her surroundings, as if seeing them for the first time.

The flowered sofa, covered with plastic, looked like an island, book-ended with wood veneer tables. The sofa also served as a let-out bed for Ross. The five girls had two of the three bedrooms upstairs. There was hardly enough room for the six children already in the family. *Where would we put a baby?*

One thing everyone said about the Smalls family, was that their housekeeping standards were always above average for a large family. The beds were always made, the sweeper was run every day, the dishes were always done, and the kitchen floor was mopped every night.

Jackie slammed the screen door and returned to her crate. This time, she didn't mingle with the crowd.

Annette sashayed over to where Jackie had plunked her

hips and said, "What's wrong with you, Jackie?" her teasing voice interrupting Jackie's reverie. "C'mon and dance. You the queen of disco."

"Aw, disco is out," Jackie scoffed. She turned her back, squared her shoulders, then twisted her mouth into a frown, so everyone would know to leave her alone.

Chapter 2

The smell of smoke, charcoal and lighter fluid, and the sounds of blood sizzling on the grill made Jackie want to cover her mouth and retch again. The beat of the music, the thump of the boogieing feet, and the bright colors of the dancers, twirling around the yard like Hawaiian lanterns made her feel as if she was inside a kaleidoscope.

In her struggle to keep from barfing again, she managed to swallow the bile forming in her throat. Tears scorched her eyes.

Suddenly, Mrs. Smalls caught Jackie in her line of vision.

Jackie thought she would die, and seemed to catch her breath in the nick of time. The young girl's heart *kabumped* and beat so loudly, she could swear her mother could hear it from across the yard. Trying to appear calm, she sucked in her stomach.

Her mother's absent-minded gaze hovered momentarily, alighted on Jackie, then skipped over her like a butterfly flitting from flower to flower. Mrs. Smalls' dead stare settled on their apartment's back door with its one stoop.

Once her mother's X-ray vision slid past her, Jackie let out a breath. She was glad she was wearing a loose T-shirt today.

Jackie studied Mrs. Smalls under her long eyelashes. She thought her mother seemed a little nervous, from the way she kept wiping sweat from her forehead, shaking her head, and sighing. But that was Mom. She always was a worrywart.

Jackie sure was glad she didn't take after her mother's uptight nature. She just wanted to dance and have fun.

Out of the corner of her eyes, Jackie examined her mother some more.

Turning the ribs and chicken on the grill, Mom's brow cut a slash in her face. It furrowed in worry so.

The truth was, Jackie wasn't so much concerned about her mother's well-being as she was about herself. Had Mom guessed her secret? Mom usually checked the sanitary napkin box every month, but she seemed to have overlooked that Jackie hadn't asked for any female products for two months straight. The nurse said she was about six weeks pregnant.

Luckily for Jackie, her mother always seemed a little anxious and distracted, ever since her father had decided to sell his corner-store business and was making trips back and forth to North Carolina.

"I'll send money home to take care of the children," she'd overheard her father say to her mother a number of times, when they were arguing in their bedroom in the early hours of the morning.

A thought hit her. Jackie wondered what it would be like not to have her father in the home. Although Jackie was proud to have both parents, sometimes she couldn't stand the tense periods between them. So many of the children in the projects didn't have fathers who lived at home with them that it made her feel special whenever she said, "my dad," or people said, "I seen your pops. He look like he don't play." She would beam inside.

Today, though, an undercurrent of tension gripped the yard, and Jackie couldn't get in the flow, couldn't quite put her finger on what was going on between her parents.

Besides, the truth of the matter was Jackie's real reason for studying her mother in such detail was so that she could figure out the best time to break the bad news to her.

She'd denied all the signs to herself, the sore breasts, the frequent urination, and the morning sickness, but there was one thing she couldn't deny. The pregnancy test she'd taken at the free clinic a week ago was positive.

Jackie, just turning sixteen, was going to be a mother, without the benefit of a husband. In fact Kenny, the baby's father, had started distancing himself from her.

When the nurse handed her the results, Jackie's toes and fingers turned into icicles. Goose bumps invaded her arms. She imagined the palpitations in her chest to be the same type of arrhythmia one would experience before having a heart attack.

The nurse was blunt and to the point. "Are you going to keep it?"

Jackie had been too dazed to answer. The blood rushing through her heart pounded as loudly as the oilrigs she'd seen on the La Brea hills once, while on a field trip with her elementary school. Her palms were clammy with sweat. She didn't know what she was going to do.

Even if she wanted to do something, she didn't have two hundred dollars to pay for an abortion. She couldn't ask her mother either, because then she'd have to tell her what the money was for. And at any rate, as far as she knew, her mother didn't believe in abortion anyhow.

When Jackie saw Kenny at school the following day, she told him, "You're going to be a daddy."

Kenny responded like his hands hadn't been all over her. Like his lips hadn't left monkey bites on her neck so dark that she had to wear high-collared blouses for weeks to hide the marks from her parents?

"How do I know it's mine?"

Puh-lease.

Kenny's words came back to haunt her. Just remembering the cold stare he'd given her, a chill caterpillared up her spine.

Now with Kenny denying paternity, once again, she felt abandoned, alone, and afraid. And as if that wasn't bad enough, it appeared as if her father was getting ready to leave the family.

For the whole week she had cried. How could she tell her mother? Now all the lies she'd told about running to school dances and being with her girlfriends were about to catch up with her. She thought of all the days she'd skipped school and wished she could take it all back.

Once again, an undertow began roaring in her stomach, before washing over her in a wave of regret.

Why didn't she use protection?

Oh, Lord, what was I thinking about?

That momentary pleasure could not make up for the tenderness in her breasts, the queasiness in her stomach, or the heartburn in her throat.

She didn't think she could get pregnant, even though she had been sexually active for a year and was taking more and more risks.

She thought back to the night she'd first slept with Kenny.

Kenny knew, once his mother was asleep, he could sneak Jackie up the back stairs to his room, which was in the attic.

Earlier that night, Jackie had gone to the club with Annette, who'd just been given permission to go to teenage nightclubs. Jackie pleaded and cajoled until her mother gave in and said she could go with Annette.

Meantime, while Annette was dancing, Jackie and Kenny decided to sneak out of the club to go to his house.

Everything went as planned . . . until they fell asleep and didn't make it back to the club on time.

Annette waited for a half-hour, after everyone had filed out of the club. The guard told Annette that the club was empty, yet there was still no sign of Jackie. Annette was forced to leave the club alone. Good thing Jackie's girlfriend, Lisa, waited outside with her.

After an hour, Lisa drove Annette home.

"I don't know what I'm going to tell my Moms and Pops," Annette moaned.

"Just say you saw her leave with another girl," Lisa suggested.

"Oh, I'm in deep trouble, fooling with this girl. I could kick her behind." Annette knew she was going to be held responsible for her younger sister.

When she arrived home around 12:30, her mother was waiting up for her, as usual.

Her father later joined the two in the kitchen, clutching the edge of the old-fashioned sink, veins standing prominently in his neck. "Where is Jackie, Annette?"

Annette froze up. Her father had never hit her, and she didn't want this to be the first time. She had never felt afraid of her father before, but looking at the fierce glare on his face, suddenly she was petrified. Even the sunflowers in the kitchen curtains seemed sinister and threatening.

"I don't know."

Her mother's face drew into a tightly drawn persimmon knot. "You're lying, Annette," her mother said. "I expect more from you than this. You know, as the oldest, you have to set the example. Do you want all your sisters to start running wild?"

"Why would you leave your younger sister out in the streets like that?" her father asked. "You know it's dangerous out there. Nothing better happen to your little sister, or I'm going to be on you like white on rice."

Annette lied because she was afraid of her parents and because she was covering for Jackie. She had never been in this situation before; she didn't date yet, and she seldom went to parties.

Annette's parents grilled her over and over, catching her in one lie after another.

Finally she broke down in tears. "I don't know where she's at."

Mr. Smalls raised his voice louder than he ever had before when speaking to Annette, who, up till now, was always the obedient, compliant child. "What? You don't know where your baby sister is at?"

"I'm sorry, Daddy. I just don't know where she went."

"Well, nothing better not happen to that girl, or I'm going to hold you responsible."

Mrs. Smalls intervened. "Don't say that, honey. Jackie's going to be fine. I know it. We'll just pray about it."

What seemed like twenty-four hours later, but was actually two hours later, Jackie came waltzing in at 2:30 a.m., without so much as a "fare-thee-well," as Mr. Smalls put it.

Her mother, father, and sister were waiting for her at the door.

"Where have you been?" Mrs. Smalls demanded, arms akimbo, on her slender, shapely hips. "Annette's been here for two hours."

Jackie was silent. She couldn't even think of a reasonable lie.

"What are you doing, Jackie? You better not bring no little crumbsnatchers in here to feed. I'll put you out if you do." Her father's voice had never been so threatening. He usually left the disciplining to their mother.

Jackie's eyes widened in fear, her throat clamped shut.

Their heads hung, Jackie and Annette stood before their parents, while their father and mother yelled back and forth, waking up the rest of the house.

Finally, her father said, "You and Annette are on punishment for a month. Only school, home, and church, you hear?"

When they stumbled into the bedroom they shared, Annette started in on Jackie. "See, Jackie, now look what you've done. We're both grounded. I could kick your butt myself." Annette pounded her fist into her palm. "You're just too fast and too hardheaded. Did you do anything with that boy? You know they only want one thing."

Even under the cover of the darkened room, Jackie kept a straight face. She felt she had to act, think, and believe her lie herself. She acted as if she wasn't doing anything different than her other sisters.

"No, we didn't do anything."

Jackie cringed from the memory.

Now the truth would come out. Everyone would know she had been sexually active and "fast," just like the neighbors always thought she was. They often judged her by the provocative way she dressed and because she wore lipstick from the time she was twelve years old.

Several of the older neighborhood women had approached her mother once.

"We don't like Jackie's attitude around boys," Miss Cleondra said. "She seems a little too fresh for a young girl."

"Oh, she's just high-spirited," Wylene said, defending her daughter.

Never mind the stares and whispers, Jackie hated that she had let her mother down.

Although there were other young girls in the neighborhood who had babies, Jackie knew her family was considered better than that. Now she felt like she was about to bring disgrace on the family.

Now today, for a holiday, there seemed to be a lot of tension.

Nervously, Jackie glanced over at her father. He seemed real distant and isolated from everyone. He was not drinking his usual cold beer, or playing "bones" (dominoes) with his cronies.

"C'mon, Eric, let me whip you in a game of bones," Wild Bill called out to Mr. Smalls.

Mr. Smalls shook his head and stomped into the house.

Jackie felt uneasy, but didn't think her father was mad at her. She'd heard her father and mother arguing late into the night for the last month.

"Jackie, watch the meat." Mrs. Smalls tore off her barbecue sauce-stained apron.

Jackie trundled over to the pit, weaving through the crowd, tightening her stomach muscles.

Her mother handed her the fork and, without looking at her, spun on her heels and headed to the house.

Jackie's stomach felt so queasy, she could hardly stand the charcoal smell and the sight of the purple juices oozing out of the chicken and ribs. Trying so hard not to vomit, she paid little attention to the loud screaming and arguing coming from inside the apartment, as bits and snatches of conversation floated out the window.

"Why would you sell the business?"

"I've given you half of the money, woman. What do you want? Blood?"

"North Carolina is too far away. Who's going to take care of your children?"

"I know these are my children. Haven't I always taken care of them?"

"We need you. It's not just the money."

"You black women don't understand_"

"What do you mean, we black women? Ain't you black? Is this about a white woman?"

The neighbors looked uneasily at one another, but continued partying.

Jackie watched her brother and Cornbread stop dancing to come over and ask for a hotdog.

"Relish?"

"Nah."

Cornbread, who always mimicked Ross, threw up his hand. "Nah."

Annette sidled up to Jackie, cupped both hands about her ears and whispered, "I wonder what Moms and Pops are arguing about?"

Swallowing her vomit, Jackie shrugged her shoulders.

The next thing she knew, her father slammed out the apartment door, suitcase in hand.

Wylene, who was on his heels, cried out, "Where are you going?" She snatched at Mr. Smalls' shoulder.

For a moment, the music stopped, and everyone looked on silently.

Eyes glazed, jaw set, and without so much as a glance over his shoulder, Eric snatched his hand away from Wylene. He muttered under his breath, "I'm outta here."

Wylene began to cry uncontrollably. "Honey, you don't mean that. Come back, honey. We can work it out. We've been through worse than this." Wylene threw her arms around Eric's waist in a vise-like bear hug.

"Wylene, leave me alone, woman!" Mr. Smalls peeled her splayed fingers, like onion layers, one by one, from around his waist.

Seemingly, all in one precise motion, he jumped into his beat-up Ford, not looking back at anyone, and sped off, the car wheels screeching like a lion's roar.

Suddenly, the world fell silent. After that, everything

moved in slow motion, reminding Jackie of that child-hood game, freeze.

The only thing Jackie could see was the strange look on Ross' Hershey-colored face. He stopped eating his hot dog, then threw it down on the ground and ran into the house, lips pinched.

Apparently too afraid to follow his best friend inside, Cornbread stood frozen like an ice sculpture, his eyes glued to Ross' retreating back.

Chapter 3

Five months later . . .

Annette gazed up at the clock. It was nine o' clock at night, time for her to punch out of her after-school job at the local Parks and Recreation Center. She had to be up at six in the morning to attend school. She was in her senior year.

Her day had slowed down, and she was left alone with her thoughts. Being the eldest girl in the family, her mother had confided more in her than she did the others, and things didn't look too good right now. She wondered what was going to come of her family, now that her father had left the home. The family had just found out too that Jackie was having a baby.

When it rains, it pours.

Annette suddenly started feeling a bit depressed. She'd been so distraught about her father's leaving. Even so, she decided that she was going to hang on to her dreams of becoming a secretary with Los Angeles County. She'd heard that they paid good money and would even pay for night classes at college. Would there be enough money to make it? Since she could type 50 words per minute, Annette was confident she'd be able to find work after graduation.

Working at the community center was her first part-time job as a secretary, but she only made minimum wage. She turned all but her school money over to the household.

A girl named Peaches, who attended the same high school, came up to her. "Hey, Annette, I heard your sister's pregnant. Is it true?"

Annette turned away and didn't answer.

Peaches threw her hand up. "Forget you, with your old stuck-up self. That's what y'all Smalls get. Think y'all better than everybody."

Annette was so angry that she couldn't speak. She couldn't believe how people from the projects could be so heartless and cold. She picked up her purse and got ready to walk the four blocks home. Even though her neighborhood was as rough as they come, she wasn't afraid because she'd grown up there and knew most of the people.

She knew that people in the neighborhood all *thought* that Jackie was fast, but as far as she knew, until she found out about the pregnancy, Jackie wasn't sexually active.

Her father and mother had kept a tight rein on all of the Smalls' girls. At seventeen and a half, she was still a virgin. And with Mr. Smalls' absence, the girls were more determined than ever to stay chaste and make something out of their lives.

Sometimes Annette wondered how she'd never noticed that Jackie wasn't menstruating. Then she remembered that Jackie used to ask for sanitary napkins, when the other girls did. Of course, they all respected each other's privacy and didn't check each other's pads after disposal.

"That girl is no sneaky," Annette said out loud to the night air. She pulled up her collar. Now she figured that Jackie had probably lied the night that she'd stayed out late last year.

Because Annette didn't sneak around and lead a double-life, she'd just assumed that Jackie was like her. After all, they'd been raised in the same household, where her mother always said, "Men want to marry virgins. Don't sell yourself short."

Even so, Jackie was her sister, and blood was thicker than mud. *How dare Peaches try to put my baby sister down!*

The following day . . .

"Central Ave," the heavy-set bus driver called out.

Jackie was so drowsy that she had dozed off completely. She jerked her head away from the half-opened bus window, where she was nodding and slobbering. The first thing that leaped into her consciousness was the bus driver's shave bumps and the rolls of fat on the back of his neck and head.

Gross!

She tried to get rid of a sudden feeling of nausea, swallowing a glob of saliva. She felt like spitting all the time. Her mother had told her that some women stayed nauseated throughout their entire pregnancy. She guessed she was one of them.

Jackie remembered her mother going from being upset at finding out that she was pregnant to being concerned that she hadn't received any prenatal care up until six months.

After Mrs. Smalls took her daughter to the clinic, she was relieved when the doctor said that the baby was developing normally and that Jackie was as healthy as could be.

Sometimes Jackie didn't understand her mother. One thing was for sure though. She had no idea that being pregnant could make her this tired. How did her mother bear six children? She didn't think she'd ever get pregnant again. She was so miserable, she could hardly stand to put one foot in front of the other, to keep breathing, to keep moving.

Out of the corner of her eyes, she glanced at the carefree young girls wearing biker shorts and high-top gym shoes, laces wrapped around their muscular legs, teasing and jostling each other, as they stood in the aisle on the bus.

"Hey, Takisha," one girl shouted, "I saw your boyfriend with that new girl in English."

"You a lie. He was with me."

"Girl, you crazy."

A loud roar of raucous laughter filled the bus.

Oh, how Jackie wished she could change places with them. She wished she could pick herself a new boyfriend, with all she had to worry about.

Kenny. Her baby's father popped into her mind.

The last time she saw him at school, he'd put his arm

around the slender waist of his new girlfriend, Chyna, and turned away.

Hot tears sprang to her eyes as she thought about what Annette had told her about her Kenny. (The day before, Annette had seen him at the hamburger hangout with Chyna.) "He said he doesn't believe the baby is his, because you didn't tell him."

Jackie heaved a sigh. There would be no help forthcoming from him. She was so sickened at the sight of him. Now she wondered what she ever saw in him. As if it wasn't bad enough that her father had left the family, now her baby's father had walked out on her too.

After six months, all of the members of the Smalls family still seemed depressed about their father's absence. Hardly anyone talked about him too much, and an unspoken sadness seemed to cover the whole family.

Personally, Jackie's world had never felt colder.

She remembered Miss Cleondra saying to her one day, "That's what you get for trying to be so grown."

Well, if this was what being grown was, she didn't like it. Not one bit. She thought about all the things her mother had warned her against. *Why didn't I listen?*

It had only been three weeks since Jackie's mother found out through the school nurse that she was pregnant, so now she attended a maternity school with other teenaged mothers-to-be in midtown L.A. Every day she had to commute for an hour back and forth across L.A.'s many ethnic neighborhoods.

Now, it seemed as though the world was made up of two sets of people—the young, who had prom to look forward to, and the others left holding the bag, like her, who had no future to consider.

She looked at all the young teenage boys on the bus, pants sagging, jheri curls swinging, and her stomach turned. Since she was visibly pregnant, they no longer made cat-calls at her. Even adults would look at her taut skin and peach-shaped face and then avert their gaze. It was as though she was invisible, in spite of her stomach, which resembled a basketball.

Since she'd left regular school, it seemed as though her stomach had popped out even more. In a way, though, she was relieved to no longer have to hide her pregnancy.

For six months, Jackie hid her stomach from her family, her friends, and her teachers by wearing tight girdles and sucking in her stomach. When the baby started moving, she was surprised that no one saw the little legs and arms sticking up. For those six months, she pretended to have a period when her sisters did, and Mrs. Smalls was too dis-tracted to notice.

Jackie even started wearing Ross' baggy clothes.

Annette used to tease her. "You're getting to be a tom-boy, Jackie. Whatever happened to my sister, the diva?"

In dismissal, Jackie would flip Annette a birdie.

After six months, Jackie's big clothes were barely hiding the bulge, which was rising higher and higher above her navel. Somehow, she still couldn't find the right time to tell her mother, so she hid it, until her English teacher no-ticed and told the school nurse.

Through all of what was going on, Jackie knew she hadn't menstruated since her father left, but she didn't want to burden her mother with more worries.

Mr. Eric Smalls had sold his store, given his wife half of the money, and promised to keep sending money every month for as long as he was gone. The store didn't net too much money from its sale, and the stash Mr. Smalls gave his wife was gone in the first two months, with their mother trying to feed six children.

Jackie sensed Mrs. Smalls had a gut feeling about what was going on, but she didn't think her father was man enough to say what he wanted to do. Which was to never return home to his family. Jackie, who now knew how it felt to be heartbroken, intuitively understood that her mother cried and cried when she was alone, although Mrs. Smalls never let her children see her real emotions.

Jackie thought back to when her dad lived at home and the O.G.'s (Original Gangsters) from the project's would tell the younger, up-and-coming gang members, "Homey, don't mess with that little, fast Smalls' sister. She jail bait. Her pops look like he don't play that shit."

Jackie thought about it. She comforted herself that at least no one from the projects could claim they had bust her cherry, which didn't matter now no way. Pregnant was still pregnant. Now with her dad gone, she no longer felt safe and protected.

Weeks had passed by and at first, the Smalls children were asking more and more about their dad. Slowly, without a word or any money from Mr. Smalls, the weeks turned to months. The children had accepted what was going on and, because of what he was putting their mother through, didn't want to see or speak to him anyway.

Finally, Mrs. Smalls had to sit all of the children down and tell them the truth, not Mr. Smalls' version, but hers. "Your dad has left us. He won't be back."

Annette tried to soften the blow. "Don't worry, Mom, as

soon as I graduate, I'll get a full-time job and help on the bills. Meantime, I'll use my after-school job to help where I can. I'll buy all my senior pictures and class ring, and the rest will go to the household. I won't be going to prom, so I won't have that expense."

Ross, who'd just started working as a checkout boy at the local grocery store, added, "I'll start giving you my check from Wu Tsing's." Ross used to work in his own father's store, and quickly learned the difference between having a family business and being someone else's employee.

Since Wylene could no longer count on Mr. Smalls sending her money, she went to apply for state assistance. She'd always prided herself on never having to take public assistance, but these were tough times. She also knew it was time to look for a job.

She found one at an elementary school, where she was hired as a teacher's assistant. Fortunately for Mrs. Smalls, her minimum-wage job did not interfere with her Aid to Dependent Family and Children's check or her food stamps.

Meantime, Jackie still hadn't found the right time to tell her mother and hated that her mother had to hear it from a stranger.

Jackie thought back to that morning in late November, when her English teacher, Ms. Gilbert, called her to the front of the room and handed her a folded, white piece of paper. "Take this to the school nurse."

Jackie lifted her eyebrow, sucked her stomach in, then walked back to her desk and picked up her books and notebook.

When she arrived at the nurse's office, another female student was in the room.

"Step inside my office," Mrs. Coleman told her, without breaking her stride with the other student. She continued wrapping the student's wrist in a bandage. "I'll be right with you."

Ten minutes later, when she was done with the other student, Mrs. Coleman went straight to the point. "When is it due, Jackie?"

Jackie dropped her head. "March."

"Does your mother know?"

Jackie shook her head.

"What's your mother's number?"

"She's at work."

"What's the number at your home? I'll call her tonight."

Jackie complied. She felt so low that she wanted to sink into the ground. She started to think, *If only* . . . Then she had to catch herself. There was no way to change the present.

Since her father had left, Jackie often heard her mother crying at night, when she thought the children were asleep, so the last thing she wanted to do was bring more pain and worry to her mother's doorstep.

Now even with her new job, Mrs. Smalls was barely making ends meet. She simply couldn't feed six children on her income.

Jackie thought about it. Annette and Ross were working part-time to help out, and she felt bad that she was the only one who would not be able to work. She felt even worse about her predicament.

How could we afford to feed another mouth?

Not only was she bringing shame and disgrace on the family, she was going to add economic hardship to an already strapped situation.

Fortunately, her mother didn't get home from her teacher's aide job at the local elementary school until four, and Jackie hoped that she would get home before Mrs. Coleman called.

Jackie rushed home from school, hoping to get there before her mother received the phone call from Mrs. Coleman. She had made up her mind that she should be the first to inform her mother.

Meanwhile, back at Compton High, Mrs. Coleman was dialing Jackie's English teacher, Mrs. Gilbert.

"Hello, Mrs. Gilbert, this is Norma."

"Oh, hi. How are you?"

"I'm good. Listen, I saw that young lady you sent today with the note, and I want to thank you for stepping in. She happens to be six months pregnant."

"I'm not surprised. I happened to get a good look at her today. I couldn't believe my eyes . . . and to think that she's been sitting in my class all this time."

"Don't be too hard on yourself. I mean, your hands are full already trying to keep up with the curriculum."

"You know, I thought she was having problems in the home or something, because she's been a little withdrawn over the last couple of weeks or so. I feel like I let her down, not finding out sooner."

"Yeah, but you're not the parent. How could she be so far pregnant and her mother not notice? I mean, she's got to leave the house every day in that condition."

"You're right."

"Well . . . that leaves me now with a very awkward phone call to make. I'll be calling her mother right after I get off the phone with you. You know, this is the part of the job I hate the most, breaking this kind of news to an unsuspecting parent."

"I could well imagine."

"Who knows how far this would have gone if you didn't—"

"I might have been calling a midwife instead."

"Anyway, thanks again for keeping your eyes open. You might have saved a life . . . or two."

"No problem. Talk to you later."

Mrs. Coleman sighed heavily after hanging up. It would be the third phone call of the kind she'd be making for the school year. She clutched her cup of coffee and took a long swig. She decided to get it over with once and for all.

She started shuffling papers on her desk, which was cluttered with a lot of paperwork. "I just had it here," she said to herself. "Ah, here it is." She dialed the number to Jackie's home.

"Hello."

"Mrs. Smalls, I am Norma Coleman, the nurse at your daughter's school. Do you have a minute? I'd like to discuss something with you."

"Okay. What happened? Jackie fell ill?"

"No. She's fine."

Then there was an awkward silence.

"Mrs. Smalls, your daughter is pregnant." Norma Coleman didn't know of any better way to communicate than to simply tell her.

"What! Pregnant? No, no, no, this can't be right. Are we talking about Jackie Smalls?"

"Yes, ma'am. I'm sorry. She had a visit with me today upon the recommendation of a teacher. Turns out she is six months pregnant."

"I don't know what to say . . . I-I-I been warning that girl to stay out of trouble. How could that happen? She doesn't even have a boyfriend."

"You were young once, remember? You know, kids get into all kinds of stuff, and usually the parents are the last to find out."

Mrs. Smalls broke out into a cold sweat and started shaking nervously. "Is there anything we can do?"

"Besides support her, I'm afraid not. Jackie is too far into her pregnancy."

Mrs. Smalls was weeping uncontrollably now. Her whole world was crumbling before her very eyes. And some part of her was hoping that it wasn't true, that there was some kind of mistake.

"Mrs. Smalls, I know this is very hard for you, but you and your husband have to sit with her and the baby's father to sort out this situation. I know this may be small consolation, but a lot of people have worked around teenage pregnancy and have bounced back. This is not the end. She's young and bright, and she's got her whole future ahead of her. In fact there is a school for teenage mothers-to-be, and she can continue her education there."

"You don't understand. Her father no longer lives here, and I have five other children to take care of."

"Wow! I guess the contact information needs to be updated." Norma Coleman put a check mark on Jackie's file. "So that makes it that much harder."

"I've been so busy these days since their father up and

left, working full-time and all, I feel kind of responsible for the whole thing."

"Please . . . Mrs. Smalls it's too late now to beat up on yourself. Sometimes, even when you do your best, things can still go wrong. As a matter of fact I made a similar call three weeks ago and both parents lived in the home, were professionals, the whole bit. You know, you can't always control what your kids do."

Her face drenched with tears, Mrs. Smalls tried to dry her eyes. "That's true."

A long period of silence cut right through the call.

"Mrs. Smalls, you there?"

"Yes, I'm here."

"I have to get off the phone right now, but I'll be calling you tomorrow to see how you're doing. Remember, Jackie needs you more than ever now."

"Okay, I'm gonna bear that in mind. And thanks for being there for me. I really needed a shoulder to cry on."

"Ah . . . don't mention it. It comes with the territory."

"Thanks again."

"Bye now."

As soon as Jackie walked in the door, she knew from the sad look on her mother's face that it was too late. *Dam. Looks like Mrs. Coleman got to Mom first.*

"I guess we'll just have to make way for another mouth to feed," was all her mother said. The way Mrs. Smalls' face crumpled, and her shoulders heaved, it was worse than any whipping she could have put on Jackie.

Wylene shuffled off to her bedroom, where she remained until dinner. Jackie went to her bedroom, too, where she stayed without going down to eat.

As much as she was saddened to bring this "new burden" on her family, Jackie was still very much relieved. She no longer had to hold her breath and hide her pregnancy. Wearing clothes two sizes too big, and making the most of some old-fashioned girdles at the second-hand store, she was growing tired of hiding her stomach.

Now she could breathe. She was even surprised at how much her stomach popped out, when she wasn't holding it in.

"Why didn't you tell me?" Annette said to her that night when she went to bed.

Jackie didn't say anything. She was stunned. Obviously, her mother had already told Annette.

"I could've gotten you some birth control pills at the clinic."

"I thought you didn't believe in pre-marital sex."

"I don't. But I believe less in a sixteen-year-old mother trying to take care of a baby."

"Fine time to tell me now."

"Don't worry, girl. You my sister, and I'm gonna help you with the baby. We'll help while you go back to school."

Jackie dropped her head, trying to hide her tears. She swallowed the lump in her throat. "Thanks."

Annette gave a light laugh and hugged Jackie's slumped shoulders. "Just don't be bringing no more crumbsnatchers in here . . . with your fast self."

Chapter 4

A rich baritone voice interrupted Jackie's reverie. "May I help you, miss?"

Just as she struggled to push her swollen middle up, a young man with deep-set, burrowing eyes gave her a hand to help hoist her up from her seat near the front of the bus.

Pushing her hand into the square of her back, Jackie said, "Thanks." She waddled to the middle of the bus, to get off on the back exit. This way she could avoid the crowds climbing in and bum-rushing the seats at the front door.

When she reached for the door handles, she noticed the same tawny hand push the swinging door open. Jackie refused to look up at the helping hand though. The sun hit her with a blinding glare, causing her to squint and cover her eyes to catch her bearings.

Jackie continued walking, not looking back.

Just when she had gotten a block away from the bus stop, a voice called behind her, startling her. Goose bumps rose on her arms, and she felt her heart quicken with fear. *You could never be too careful in this neighborhood.*

"Wait up. Let me carry your books."

Jackie gazed up to see the same young man who had helped her on the bus. He sported a jheri curl, just like her brother, only his hung shoulder-length. It made her think of the Bible account of Samson, whose strength was in his hair.

To keep the sun out of her eyes, Jackie squared her free hand over her brows. "That's okay." She continued walking, hoping the stranger would go on his way.

"Look, that might be too much strain on your back, with the baby and all."

Jackie spun around and took a good look at this Good Samaritan.

The young man stared directly in her eyes. His eyes were chestnut brown and reminded Jackie of a panther's, the way they seemed to penetrate her tough facade.

After so much rejection, she couldn't believe he was still trying to talk to her. He looked a little older than Kenny and could've been perhaps nineteen or twenty.

Jackie, left arm akimbo, books tucked under her right arm, rolled her head on her neck, eye whites showing, then curled her lips in a sneer. "Don't you see I'm pregnant? What's wrong with you?"

The young man threw back his head and let out a hearty laugh. "And what has that got to do with anything? You're a beautiful young woman. Please let me help you carry your school bag."

Suddenly, the baby began kicking and tied up in a knot. Jackie bent over to catch her breath.

"Miss, are you all right?"

Jackie drew in a deep breath. When she felt his hand, ever so gently, touch her neck, she hesitated for a split second, but the sincere look of concern in his eyes made her change her mind.

As she straightened up, she slowly relented and handed over her books. "Yes, I'm okay. The baby just moved." The way the young man cocked his head to the side reminded her of Ross.

"What's your name? Mine's Roger." The young man fell into step with her, with his easy, long-legged lope.

"I don't just give my name out to everybody. How do I know if you're not a gangbanger. I don't have time for no foolishness."

"Look, I'm coming from The Job Center that's near here in Downing. I live down in the jungle though."

"Where's 'the jungle'?" Jackie asked. She'd never been outside of the projects before she started going to the maternity school.

"It's down off Santa Barbara Boulevard and La Cienega." Roger added, "Anyhow, they say I may be getting a job by the end of the week. Where are you coming from?"

"You sure ask a bunch of questions."

"I just want to get to know you better. Is that all right?" Roger gave her that sidelong grin.

Jackie felt herself relax. Even though Roger's easy stride had a small dip in it, it wasn't a gangbanger's walk.

As they walked into the projects, Jackie noticed the gossipy neighbors pointing at her, but suddenly she didn't care.

For the first time in months, she felt young and buoy-ant. It wasn't that she was attracted to Roger. She was just happy to have someone to talk to who didn't look away from her. At last, someone saw her as a human being and not a "fast young girl who was having a baby." He looked directly in her eyes, whenever he spoke, and made her feel beautiful.

He walked her up to her front door, then bowed at the waist as she went in the house.

She pivoted around on one foot.

Roger quizzically lifted one eyebrow and tilted his head to the side. "What?"

"Name's Jackie."

"I like that name."

"Thanks." Smiling inwardly, Jackie closed the door, hugging the books close to her heart.

The following morning, Jackie saw Roger when he bounced onto the bus, skipping all but one step. She no-ticed he was whistling, and it made her think of her father during happier times.

He looked around the bus, piercing the crowd of rowdy teens, then walked directly to where Jackie was sitting at the back of the bus.

Jackie scooted over.

"Hi, Jackie. Do you like Twinkies?"

Jackie wondered how he knew she craved Twinkies all the time. She nodded.

When he produced a Hostess Twinkie, Jackie was hooked.

They talked all the way until he got off the bus.

From that day forth, each morning and evening, she

would look forward to seeing Roger. Now she didn't mind going to school.

Talking about their problems, Jackie found out that Roger was twenty, was on parole from Tehachapi Prison, but was serious about finding a job as a forklift operator.

Somehow, Roger managed to land a job at an Evans Warehouse in San Pedro within a week of meeting Jackie.

He told her, "Let's go celebrate."

Even though they didn't call it a date, they went out after school that evening and ordered hamburgers.

For the first time, Jackie found out what it felt like to become friends before lovers, and she began to enjoy the relationship. Roger would bring her little gifts, such as chewing gum, greasy-spoon hamburgers, since she craved the greasy onions, and hand-packed ice cream cones.

Still, Jackie hadn't introduced Roger to her family yet. She didn't know how they would take it, with her being pregnant by one guy and going out with another. Actually, they weren't really going out. They were just enjoying each other's company.

One afternoon as she neared her old high school, Jackie saw Kenny clamber onto the bus, accompanied by his new girlfriend, Chyna.

He dropped down in a seat near the front, his arm around her. As soon as they sat down, they began tongue kissing.

Jackie, traveling alone that day because Roger had to work overtime, turned her head, averted her gaze, and stared out the window. She decided to act like she didn't see him. Out of the corner of her eye, though, she saw Kenny whisper something in Chyna's ear.

Kenny got up and, with his long-legged stride, holding

on to the back of seats, jostled through the throng of students standing on the bus. He made his way over to Jackie. "Hey, Jackie."

Jackie grimaced as if in real pain. "Hey."

"You sure are big. You sure they ain't twins?"

"Yeah, whatever." Jackie acted nonchalant. She no longer cared for Kenny, but just seeing him with the other girl turned her stomach. *Another sucker*, she thought. She wondered if he was using a jimmy this time. She put her books in front of her stomach.

"If it's mine, I'm gon' take care of it."

Jackie paused and gave him the evil eye. "What do you mean, if it's yours? Forget you, Kenny. You don't have to do nothin' for this baby."

One morning around 8 a.m. in early March, when Jackie put on her school clothes to get ready for class, water gushed down her legs and left a puddle at her feet. By this time, Mrs. Smalls had already left for her job and Jackie had no idea what was going on.

Annette turned to her and said, "You're going to have that baby today. I'll call in to work."

The week before, Jackie had gone to the clinic, and the obstetrician said that the baby wouldn't be due for about three more weeks. She had planned to go to school up until at least a week before her due date, and that particular day, she wanted to take a test. Although she wasn't sure what was happening, from what she'd read in her prenatal books, she suspected her labor was imminent.

At first, the pains were mild cramps, but by afternoon, the twinges had turned into sharp piercing pains.

Jackie, in tears, called her mother at work, "Mom, come

home. I don't know what's happening. Water is running down my legs, and I saw a little bit of blood when I went to the bathroom."

"Calm down, Jackie. The baby's probably going to be born today. Stop crying. This is your first baby, and it will probably take a while. You're a woman now. Go take a quick shower."

Jackie complied, wondering why her mother would tell her to take a shower at a time like this.

About one hour later, Mrs. Smalls finally made it home from work. She paid Miss Ernestine to drive them to Martin Luther King Hospital, where Jackie was scheduled to deliver. Jackie had gone to the local county clinic for prenatal care for the last three months. There the staff scolded Jackie and her mother for waiting so late into her pregnancy to seek medical attention. But to their surprise, the doctor said that both mother and baby were healthy.

Everything happened in a fog after that. All Jackie could remember was screaming, crying, peeing, passing gas, and sweating. She remembered the nurse putting a white gown with the back out on her, and she remembered a series of hands poking, probing, digging inside her, making her glad she had taken the shower.

She was in so much pain, she didn't even have time to be embarrassed. She just wanted what felt like an elephant stepping on her anus and a train running up the spine of her back to be over with. She cried and hollered.

"Can't you give her something?" Mrs. Smalls asked Doctor Kim, the pretty young Chinese obstetrician, who was scheduled to deliver Jackie.

Finally, after six hours, they gave Jackie a mild sedative, and she was able to doze between contractions.

Mrs. Smalls stayed with her, but that night at six, she had to leave to check on the other children. "I'll be back before you have the baby," Mrs. Smalls assured her.

Jackie was so doped up, she didn't know what time it was, and since her pains seemed to have ceased, she nodded off. The room looked like an underwater ballet, and everyone seemed like they were part of a dream.

Jackie was awaken by a sharp series of pains. She screamed, "Doctor! Nurse!" Her screams sounded like something out of the movie, *The Exorcist.*

Just when Jackie thought she couldn't take anymore, someone covered in a white hospital garb and mask came bursting into the labor room. "Jackie, it's me, Roger. When I didn't see you on the bus, I called your house. Is it too late?"

Jackie panted and blew. "No, ahhhh! No." Tears rolled down her face from both pain and joy. She was so happy to see Roger. She knew she looked a mess, but she was still glad to have someone at her side at a moment like this, even if it wasn't the baby's father.

"Pant," Nurse Adams said. "Don't push until we tell you."

"I can't help it."

"Hold on. We don't want you to tear—"

Jackie gasped between pants. "Roger . . . you . . . didn't have to come."

Roger kissed her forehead. "Wouldn't miss it for the world, baby girl."

A white male doctor rushed in, another nurse on his heels, to help deliver the baby. They snatched the sheet up, lifted it, and spread Jackie's legs.

"Baby's head's crowning," the nurse told the male doctor.

"I don't think we'll have to do a C-section after all," the male doctor said *sotto voce* to the nurse. "Page Dr. Kim and tell her to get down here."

Without warning, another thunderbolt of pain jolted Jackie, sending electricity down her spine. This time she let out a long, piercing scream and squeezed Roger's hand. "The baby's commmming . . ."

Roger grimaced. He wiped her forehead and patted her head. "Don't worry, baby, I'm here. Everything's going to be all right."

Dr. Kim rushed in just in time to deliver Jackie's seven-pound, ten-ounce baby girl.

Chapter 5

The morning that Jackie brought the baby home from the hospital, the sun flaunted its golden glory, and the sky wore a clear azure crown. Spring gave the world a pristine, brand-new feeling, as the jacaranda bloomed in a purple haze up and down her street. Here and there a few random daffodils bobbed their yellow heads along rickety fences. The projects had a "washed clean" feel to them. The chipped paint, the graffiti, the bullet holes in the windows were overshadowed by the beauty of spring. When they drove past the yellow police cordon, which let Jackie know someone had been killed, she ignored it. She wasn't worried about it. She had new life in the car.

When they pulled up in front of her family's flat in the projects, Roger asked, "You want me to carry the baby?"

Although she felt weak, Jackie shook her head and held her daughter closer to her chest. She was grateful that

Roger had offered to pick her up from the hospital, keeping her mother from having to take off work.

Jackie felt her heart warm, and her breasts began to leak. The hospital had given her a shot to dry up her milk, but it obviously hadn't taken effect yet.

Jackie thought back to the nurse who had wheeled her to the front lobby curb at the hospital.

"You sure have a pretty baby." The nurse looked up at Roger.

Jackie started to protest. "He's—"

"Thank you, miss," Roger interrupted. "She sure is a beauty. This is daddy's little girl."

Jackie lifted her eyebrow, throwing Roger a puzzled look, then, seeing him nod his head, relaxed back into the wheelchair.

Roger helped her climb into the Chrysler.

"Where'd you get this car?" she asked, after the nurse slammed the door behind her.

"My neighbor loaned it to me. Couldn't see you and my baby coming home on the bus. Look in the bag on the floor."

Jackie looked in the bag and found four pink-and-yellow frilly dresses. Her eyes widened in amazement. They were so tiny that she couldn't believe it. "Roger, these look like doll clothes."

"These are newborns' sizes, Jackie. At least that's what the sales lady told me."

"Thank you, Roger." Tears welled in her eyes and glistened like crystal waterfalls.

On the way home, Roger stopped at a K-mart and bought the baby a car seat too. That was Jackie's first surprise. Her second surprise was when she arrived at home.

"Bring that sugar pumpkin in here," Mrs. Smalls called out as soon as Roger opened the car door for Jackie, her newborn cradled in her arms.

Jackie's knees knocked, and her legs wobbled like a newborn colt's, but she was happy to be home. She ignored the stitches, which burned her groin, and made sitting down in the car uncomfortable, if not difficult.

Yoyo, Annette, Leilani, and Tasha stood on the porch, waiting with open arms to greet their first niece and Mom's first grandchild.

When Jackie stepped inside the living room, she found a throng of her mother's friends, Miss Cleondra, Miss Ernestine, and Miss Johnnie Mae, all waiting patiently. Even Cornbread and Ross were inside, looking proud to be new uncles.

"Surprise!"

The house looked sparkling clean and had a permeating smell of Pine-Sol and bleach. An embossed pink and silver banner spanned the room. Pink and white balloons were taped to the wall, streamers criss-crossing the ceiling. A neat pile of wrapped gifts with pink and white ribbons circled the wood veneer cocktail table, and a bouquet of carnations graced the cocktail table.

Jackie could tell there was a spring-cleaning spree. Annette called it, "a disinfecting war."

Jackie had been so distraught throughout the pregnancy that she had never bought more than a few T-shirts and diapers. She was happy to see the gifts, knowing her baby would now have much-needed outfits. Other than to go to school, she had basically hidden from the neighbors, so she was surprised to see all of them standing in the living room. Even gossipy old Mrs. Fisher was there.

Mrs. Smalls sat in the most comfortable, least worn-out armchair in the living room. She patted her lap. "Bring that baby in here."

Jackie was taken aback by her mother's sudden shift from anger, shame, and worry to pure pride in her new grandbaby. All her mother's friends, especially Miss Johnnie Mae, seemed genuinely happy to see the newborn.

"Sit down, Jackie," Miss Johnnie Mae said. "Give us this baby. You don't know what to do with no baby. You just a baby yourself. This our baby."

Everyone stood around Mrs. Smalls and cooed into the small pink blanket that held Jackie's baby.

"Oh, she's a beauty."

"She looks like Jackie."

"No," Mrs. Smalls told them, "this baby is an old soul. She has her great-grandmother's eyes."

Mrs. Johnnie Mae added her two cents. "These are some gray-blue eyes. I wonder if her eyes are going to change. You can't tell right now, Wylene. Your children all got those funny-colored eyes."

Suddenly, no one seemed to care anymore that Jackie was only sixteen going on seventeen, or that she wasn't married. All they saw in the rosy cheeks of Jackie's new baby was hope for the future.

At a loss for what to do, Jackie felt as if her only purpose was to deliver the baby then sit back and let everyone else take care of it. Forlorn, she eased her aching bottom down on the sofa.

Like a father waiting to be introduced, Roger sat down by her side and patted her hand, for reassurance.

Jackie had lost twenty pounds in her three-day hospital stay. Now she looked barely twelve years old. Her natural auburn hair was pulled up into a ponytail that brushed her shoulders. Her stomach was already completely flat and she'd gone down from a size 8 to a size 6.

Looking on, Jackie didn't know what to feel. Inside, she felt strange being a mother. It was as if she was watching a movie being played out on a screen, and naturally wasn't a part of it. Everything felt surreal. *Is the baby really mine?*

The baby, whom she'd named Tamika, favored the father, Kenny, but mostly looked like Jackie. Jackie had counted all five fingers and five toes, and the doctor had given the baby a score of 10 on the Agpar scale, pronouncing Tamika to be healthy. But more so than the dried stump of her navel, it was the baby's skin color that scared Jackie. Tamika's skin was so pale that it didn't seem natural.

It so worried her that while in the hospital she asked her mother, "Mom, why is my baby so white-looking? Her father's not white."

"That's that white blood on your daddy's side. You know his grandfather was full white." Her mother's voice took on a conspiratorial tone. "She'll darken as she gets older," Mrs. Smalls assured her.

As the family gathered around Tamika, Roger stood quietly by her side, and Jackie looked on appreciatively.

Yoyo, Leilani, Tasha, and Annette fought over whose turn it was to hold the baby.

"Give her to me. I'm the oldest," Annette said, pulling rank.

"Y'all gon' spoil her," Jackie warned, still stunned over the genuine goodwill of her family and the neighbors.

Mrs. Smalls told them, "Just wait 'til she starts crying tonight. We'll see who wants to hold her then."

Ross pulled out a chair for Jackie to sit at the dinner table. "Big sister, sit down. I cooked your favorite—black-eyed peas—just for you. The baby is pretty."

Jackie was shocked at how attentive Ross was. She stared at her mother in amazement. She still couldn't get over how her mother was acting like she was happy to have the baby.

Mrs. Smalls unwrapped the baby and examined her toes and fingers. She kissed the bottom of Tamika's feet. "Jackie, she does favor you when you were a baby."

Roger, who sat by her side on the sofa, cleared his throat, coughed against his fist, then crossed his arms.

Jackie looked up at him and suddenly realized he was still waiting to be introduced.

"Mom, everyone, this is Roger. I met him while I was going to the maternity school. Mom, he's the one I told you was going to give me a ride home from the hospital. He was my coach while I was in labor too."

Roger stood up and shook hands.

"Roger, you can stay for dinner," Mrs. Smalls said. "I thank you for being there for Jackie and my new grand-baby."

Wylene Smalls had cooked fried chicken, macaroni and cheese, string beans, white potatoes, and cornbread. She'd also baked a peach cobbler—another of Jackie's favorite dishes. A pitcher of Kool-Aid sat in the middle of the table.

Ross said, "Hey, sis, you know black-eyed peas is for good luck, right?"

Annette informed him, "Black-eyed peas is for good luck at New Year's."

"Yeah, yeah. I think becoming an uncle calls for a celebration. These black-eyed peas is for the baby. Get it? New Year looks like a baby when it comes in."

Cornbread nodded.

Everyone laughed.

"Let's propose a toast to Jackie and Tamika, the first Smalls grandbaby." Annette held up her glass of Kool-Aid.

Leilani stood up and toasted. "Aye, aye."

"Cheers," Yoyo said.

Jackie felt so special. After feeling so low during her entire pregnancy, she couldn't believe it. She thought back to when Ross had found out she was pregnant and wanted to beat up Kenny, and Annette had to stop him. Jackie later found out that he and Kenny did have an actual altercation.

Unlike many of the young men in the neighborhood, Ross never wore colors to affiliate him with any gangs and always stayed neutral. As a result, even the gangs respected him. He already displayed leadership skills and could've easily been a gang leader, but he was more into leading his posse through breakdancing.

"Roger, you can sit next to Jackie," Ross said. As "the man" of the family, he always sat at the head of the table.

Everyone stood in a circle, bowed their heads, and held hands as Mom led the prayer. "Lord, we thank You for this food we are about to receive, and we thank You for Jackie making it safely through her labor. And, Lord, thank You for this new grandbaby. May God guide and protect her. Amen."

"Amen."

Roger cleared his throat as he raised his bowed head.

Without missing a beat, he went straight to the matter at hand. "Mrs. Smalls, I know you don't know me very well, but I'd like to make a proposal. I'd like to stick by Jackie and take part in baby Tammy's life. I plan to raise and treat her like she's my own child.

"I want to do whatever I can to help. I'll take care of her like she's my own. I really like Jackie and hope she will one day return the feeling."

Roger's nickname for Tamika stuck, and before long everyone was calling her Tammy.

Roger was as good as his word that he would stick by Jackie and take part in her child's life and treat her like she was his own child. He did just that by taking charge of getting Tammy's milk, Pampers, and clothes. He also made sure Jackie and Tammy had a ride to all of her doctor's appointments.

Chapter 6

The first time Roger came to the projects at night without Jackie at his side, two members of the local gang accosted him at the corner. As long as he was walking her home from school, no one ever said anything to him. They obviously assumed he was her baby's father and not a member of a rival gang, so they left him alone. But after she delivered the baby, he would have to go over to her house in the evening after he got off work. And walking alone, a young black male in Blood territory, he was seen as either a target or a threat.

The taller young man, wearing cornrows, kept his hands loosely at his side, as though he was "packing." "What set you from, cuz?"

"None. I don't bang."

Roger held his breath. He used to "bang" over five years ago, when the gangs were fighting with their fists. He'd been part of the Crenshaw Mafia and didn't want to get killed with the gats and the AK-47's the gang members were beginning to use. What helped him now was that he was twenty and looked even older.

The shorter man, who had an earring in one ear, and a designed haircut with his gang initials shaved in his head, said, "Well, we just wanted to know, 'cause niggers be gettin' smoked around here that ain't got no business up in here."

"Man, I'm just here to see my lady."

"What's her name?"

"Jackie Smalls."

"Oh, little Jackie?"

"Little fine-ass Jackie?"

"You her baby daddy?"

"Yeah."

"Okay, cool. Man, he cool. Let him go."

Roger let out a sigh of relief, when he made it to the corner.

Thinking back, Roger shook his head. *Lord, I must love this woman.*

Over the nine months they had known each other, he had never even made love to her. He'd known a time in his life when sex was the only thing he wanted from a woman, when all he wanted was physical release. But he wanted more than that with Jackie. He wanted a life, and after seeing Tammy born, he had nothing but the utmost respect for Jackie. She was like a little "Mother Earth" to him.

The baby was now going on six months, and although Roger loved Jackie, he felt like he didn't want to get hurt.

At his young age, Roger was aware of death in all things.

He'd seen many of his friends get mowed down in drive-bys and drug deals gone awry. He'd already buried a lot of "home boys," and he knew that wasn't the life he wanted for himself. At one point, he had attended so many funerals that he didn't want to go to any more services. Not even when his cousin was killed.

The last time Roger went to prison to serve a two-year sentence for B & E (breaking and entering), he'd made up his mind that when he got out he would go straight.

When he thought back to his childhood, say, from about eight, he could only say that the proliferation of drugs that came into L.A. had been a turning point and the beginning of his own downfall.

Actually, Roger became aware of drugs through his mother, Gloria, after she became hooked on PCP, which people said was a horse tranquilizer. Those "shurm" cigarettes, as his mother and her friends called them, were laced with PCP, and rendered its victims crazy.

The rest of Roger's childhood catapulted into hustle mode of trying to survive, trying to stay ahead of the Department of Public Social Services' Child Neglect Unit, trying to stay ahead of the attendance officer when he skipped so many days of school he wound up repeating eighth grade, trying not to go to Juvenile before winding up in Los Padrinos Juvenile Facility several times, trying not to wind up in a foster home, then, finally trying not to wind up in Juvenile Camp, all of this before failing eventually.

He had found out at fifteen that the mumps he'd suffered as a child had left him sterile. He couldn't have children. By the time he was sixteen, his mother died from an overdose, leaving him alone in the world.

His father had abandoned his mother, and he just felt like being with Jackie was a chance for him to be a father.

He had never told anyone about his past, until the night he told Jackie. He didn't know how she would react.

She just opened her arms and let him lay his head on her shoulder. She held him in her arms, and they both cried and cried.

Chapter 7

One afternoon, when the baby was about seven months old, a loud knock resounded at the door. Startled, Jackie glanced at the kitchen clock.

It was three-thirty, and Jackie had no idea who it could be, since she wasn't expecting anyone. Her mother and Annette, who had graduated from high school and gotten a secretarial job with Los Angeles County, were both at work. Annette even managed to buy a little cheap hooptie, which she used to take the different family members around when she wasn't working.

Mrs. Smalls usually made it home around four, and Annette didn't get in until six. Natasha, Yoyo, and Lelani were still at school as they were bused to magnet schools across town, and Ross, who was on the junior varsity basketball team, was playing a game against a school out in The Valley and wasn't going to be home until late.

Roger had just stopped by, on his way home from work. He still lived down in "The Jungle." He generally started work at 6:00 a.m. and was off by 2:30 p.m., and usually arrived at Jackie's by 3:15. He was sitting on the sofa holding the baby, and Jackie had gone to get Tamika's bottle from a pot of hot water on the stove.

Her mother didn't mind Roger coming to the house while no one was there. Mrs. Smalls seemed to intuitively sense that the relationship between Jackie and him was platonic. It really didn't matter. Whether anyone was home or not, Roger always conducted himself as a gentleman.

As Jackie tested the formula on her wrist, she called out from the kitchen, "Who is it?" She opened the door and, to her surprise, saw Kenny and his mother, Mrs. Washington, on the other side of the screen door, standing on the stoop.

A defiant slur flitted across Jackie's face. "May I help you?"

"My mother wants to see the baby," Kenny blurted out.

Jackie frowned and shook her head. Kenny was never known for having any tact.

Mrs. Washington tried to smooth over matters. "Jackie, I understand that Kenny may be the father of your baby and, if he is, I'd like to make sure he takes care of his responsibilities."

Jackie looked back at Roger, who was gently rocking Tamika, and she felt torn. She was in a quandary and didn't know what to do.

* * *

She never forgot about the fistfight between Ross and Kenny wile she was pregnant. The first time, they'd only had a verbal altercation, but when Kenny got into the second argument with Ross, generally a gentle young man, the latter had jumped tough like the rest of the projects' denizens, gesticulating wildly and throwing his hands in the air. The fight was on.

Ross asked him, "Man, you want some of this?"

They say Ross really put a whipping on Kenny.

Perhaps that's why he came by. He wants to challenge Ross again, Jackie thought.

Roger seemed gentle enough, but she knew from what he told her of his past, he'd have no problem fighting if he felt his manhood was being affronted.

In a quandary, Jackie didn't know what to say or do at first. Then, she thought about it. *Who stuck by me from the first time he'd met me while I was pregnant? Who went through the delivery with me? Who was by my side for the past seven months? And, anyhow, what makes a father? Certainly not the male, who just deposited the sperm and abandoned me.*

She thought of a TV show on Animal Planet. She remembered the lion impregnating the lioness and leaving her to rear the pride. Suddenly she felt protective of Tamika, as if she was a mother lioness.

Roger was the only father Tamika had known, so far. She'd even smiled for him already and lit up whenever she saw him.

Jackie glared at Kenny, who stood next to his mother, like the little punk he was. Then she looked back at Roger, who was being a real man in all of this.

Before she knew what came over her, she said, "That's all right. Kenny's not the father."

His mother gazed over at the baby. She clucked her tongue. "Well, she sure looks like Kenny when he was a baby. The same head, the same ears."

"All babies look alike. I don't want anything from Kenny."

Kenny gave his mother a "see-I-told-you" look, and he and his mother turned and left in a huff.

Chapter 8

"Are you sure you're over the baby's father?" Roger asked Jackie, a few nights later, while they sat in her mother's living room watching television.

Jackie arched one eyebrow, rolled her eyes, and folded her arms across her chest. For the longest time, she was silent. When she spoke, her voice was raspy with rage. "What do you think, Roger?"

Roger held the baby on his chest, gently burping her. When Tammy let out a loud belching sound, he smiled. "That's daddy's girl."

Jackie reached over and took the baby. For the first time, she felt a new emotion for her baby—*jealousy*. Was Roger just in the relationship because he wanted to be a daddy? He'd never even kissed her. She laid the sleeping baby in her bassinet, which was fast becoming too small.

"Can I ask you something?" Jackie said, her eyes lowered, her voice barely above a whisper. She could hear the loud thud of her heartbeat.

"What, Pooh Bear?"

"Do you find me attractive?" Jackie blushed, her cheeks burning with embarrassment.

"Why, yes! You're a fine little sister. Even when you were pregnant, you was catching."

"Yeah? Who?"

"Me."

"Well, why don't you act like—"

"Woman, don't you know I love you, and sometimes it's all I can do to keep my hands off you?"

"Then, why don't you ever . . . kiss me?"

Jackie no longer felt like a young girl anymore. People treated her like a grown woman now. Her mother had taken her to the clinic and gotten her a six-month supply of birth control pills. Even the neighbors treated her differently. The neighborhood boys treated her like an old woman and didn't even try to flirt with her anymore.

The irony was she hadn't had sex since she was two months pregnant, when Kenny dumped her. With the changes going on in her body throughout her pregnancy, sex was the last thing on her mind. Now it seemed that whenever people looked at her they saw a sexually active woman, when she had been celibate over a year.

Jackie had started back going to school, but then she stopped because she didn't like to be away from the baby for so many hours. "I'll get my GED," she told her mother. She didn't feel like she could fit in anymore. Everything the other teenagers talked about sounded frivolous.

* * *

Jackie faced Roger. "Roger, did you hear me?"

"It ain't no thing." Roger turned his head away and fixed his eyes on the TV set.

"What do you mean, 'It ain't no thing'? Don't I matter?" Jackie's voice faltered.

"Girl, girl, girl . . ." Roger shook his head, voice almost cracking.

Jackie was surprised to see the tears welling in his eyes.

Roger leaned over, took Jackie in his arms, and for the first time, kissed her.

Golden suns of orange and red spun around in her head. She felt her mouth opening, and the old desire, which suddenly felt brand-new, rose in her. Tears scalded her closed eyes and ran down her face, as she hungrily took Roger's tongue into her mouth.

Jackie tried to pinpoint all the emotions whirling through her. Her feelings for Roger were different than the ones she'd had for Kenny.

On the one hand, she wanted to be careful, not wanting to get hurt anymore. But the difference was Kenny was a boy, but Roger was a man and had proved it to her. He went to work every day. Then he came and sat with her until it was time for him to catch the bus home across town so that he could wake up in time for work the next morning. He was the highlight of her day, whether she admitted it to herself or not. Even Ross, who didn't like any males around his sisters, liked Roger.

Ross had gone to a football game at high school, and the girls were all gone to their various activities. Mrs. Smalls was watching TV in her bedroom.

"Let's dance, Jackie," Roger said, taking her hand and

pulling her up to her feet. He'd put the Luther Vandross tune, "If This World Were Mine."

Lifting her arms to dance with him, Jackie beamed and began to hum. She loved that song. Closing her eyes, she wrapped her arms around Roger's neck, while he encircled his arms around her, and they moved slowly across the floor.

Roger cupped her peach-shaped face in his hands, and before long, their lips found each other's again. They kissed each other greedily. It was as though they'd been waiting all their lives for that moment and couldn't get enough of each other.

"Let's go get a room, honey," he whispered in her ear, between kisses.

Jackie reached up and wiped the tears rolling down his face. "What about the baby?"

"Ask your mom if she will keep her. Let's say we're going to the movies."

Although they had to catch a bus to the Starlight Motel outside the projects, so no one in the neighborhood would see them, the only thing Jackie remembered was feeling like she was floating on a magic carpet. She might as well have been in a limousine, instead of a bus; she felt so rich.

Roger kept kissing her, down her neck, on her face, and her lips, and they held hands when they climbed off the bus.

After they lay down on the narrow bed, with its chipped red headboard, Roger began slowly undressing her. As he took off a piece of clothing, he gently kissed each part of her body. When he got down to her feet, he began slowly unlacing her sandals.

"Hurry," Jackie wanted to say, she was getting so aroused, but she remained quiet.

This was a man making love to her, not the boy Kenny who'd been so selfish.

Roger began rubbing her feet and massaging her toes. Slowly, he kissed her toes, her ankles, her calves. He took his time, kissing her, caressing her, massaging her scalp. He kissed her shoulders and worked his way down to her breasts.

By then, Jackie was squirming with anticipation.

Roger stripped down to his boxer shorts, climbed in bed next to her, and whispered, "Can you handle this?"

Jackie nodded breathlessly. She looked down under the sheet and saw that Roger had put on a condom.

"I don't want to hurt you. Are you sure it's not too soon after the baby?"

"No. The doctor said I was all healed up after my six-week checkup. The baby is seven months now."

"This is all my love. I don't have money."

"I don't care."

"My job is just minimum wage."

"Money isn't everything."

"I have a record."

"That's okay. You're a good man now."

"Do you want this?"

"Yes, baby."

"Can you take this?"

"Try me."

"I want to give you everything."

"You have."

When they woke up, it was two in the morning. Curling her toes, Jackie let out a deep sigh of contentment. She couldn't believe the difference between making love to a man and making love to a boy. Roger was so gentle and considerate.

Jackie was surprised how her vagina had closed up, almost to the same tightness she'd felt as a virgin.

They lay spooned in each other's arms, hearts pounding, breathing as ragged as seaweed, until their raging senses calmed down. A hush fell over the room then.

She thought back at how tears of pleasure rolled down her face while she held Roger, scratching his back, stroking his face, until she heard his breathing speed up and he cried out her name, braying like a trumpet. "Jackie, oh baby, Jackie, I love you!"

Roger sat up on his elbow and stared deeply into her eyes. "Baby, what are you thinking?"

Jackie, who'd felt she was so fast, so streetwise, was embarrassed. She shook her head.

"What is it?" Roger probed.

"Is this how it's supposed to be?"

"What?"

"You know . . ."

Jackie was searching for the words to explain. Something else was different. She realized now she'd never been satisfied before. She'd cried out like a flute when she reached her first orgasm, so sharp, so sweet. She felt like she'd died and gone to heaven.

"Lovemaking?"

"Yes. The woman is supposed to be satisfied too." Roger grinned. "Baby, this is really your first time then. I hate to tell you this, but you felt like a virgin."

"But I've had a baby."

"Don't matter." Roger kissed the top of her head, then threw back his head and roared with laughter. "We better get washed up and throw our clothes back on. Moms is going to be mad when we get in. I didn't mean to keep you out so late."

Jackie was surprised that her mother didn't fuss when Roger brought her home. Her family *really* liked him.

As time went on, Roger and Jackie built up a serious relationship to the point where they were ready to take another step towards being a family. Which was to move out and stay together in an apartment of their own.

One night, when they went to the movies, Roger asked Jackie if she wanted to move together.

Without hesitation, Jackie replied, "Yes."

After all, she was now almost 18. Later, she was surprised that her family did not put up any resistance to the idea.

Roger almost had a year on his job as a forklift driver. He had been renting a room at a boarding house and wanted to experience the feel of an apartment. His own apartment.

Life seemed to be working for him, and he couldn't remember feeling better about himself. He was happy with Jackie, and she seemed happy with him.

The gang members in the neighborhood had come to accept that he wasn't a rival gang member and treated him with the respect given an O.G. They left him alone.

Roger finally got a steady job at a warehouse in San Pedro. He'd saved a little money here and there, so he had his security deposit and first month's rent, which came to $900, the rent being $450.

Roger and Jackie found a clean one-bedroom apartment, not far from Jackie's mother, but it was quite empty, except for a used stove and refrigerator that came with the apartment. All they had was a bed they'd found at the Salvation Army, one wicker chair, and an old-fashioned, linoleum-topped kitchen table that Roger had built with his own hands. And they had the use of a communal laundry room.

Roger worked very hard and put in a lot of overtime, to get piece by piece, until he filled the place with an assortment of attractive, yet inexpensive, furniture. He was proud of his home, because, just as she had been trained growing up, Jackie kept the apartment neat and clean.

More and more Roger forgot about the little boy who had to fend for himself when his mother was out in the streets on drugs, accepting his new family, Jackie, Tamika, and the Smalls. In fact, Mrs. Smalls was like the mother he never really had. He addressed her as Mom.

Roger thought of his mother, whenever he thought of Jackie—His mother had him at sixteen too, and his father had taken a hike. She had boyfriends who never worked out, and often cried herself to sleep at night. He remembered her struggling, trying to make ends meet on her welfare check. Maybe that's why he wanted to be there for

Jackie. He didn't want to see that type of disaster happen to Jackie.

One day (he had to be about eight) his mother seemed to have given up. That's when she began to get high. Before, she had been the best mother, but then she started using marijuana then graduated to smoking shurm cigarettes—PCP. (In 1984, PCP was running rampant and had been for a few years.) She'd gotten caught up in the drug culture while he was growing up. He'd seen her go from a responsible mother to being less than human. She was committing slow suicide, which wound up in her final overdose.

Chapter 9

February 1985

Monday morning the Santa Ana blew in, windy and brisk, lifting a chill off the Pacific Ocean. Men bustled back and forth on Evans Warehouse dock in San Pedro, and with the wind tugging at their jackets and pushing at their backs, they almost seemed like part of a live machine.

Looking about, Roger uttered a sigh of contentment. He liked being a part of the "working man's machinery," as he liked to think of it. He was so happy to have his forklift job, he arrived at work a half-hour early nearly every day. Even though his workday started at 6:00 a.m., he would generally arrive at 5:30 a.m. In fact, everyone thought he was a model employee.

He was sitting in the cafeteria, blowing his coffee, when a voice interrupted him.

"Hey, G, why you always whistling?" Melvin, a fellow worker, asked him.

Roger was such a happy man that he couldn't help whistling, especially when he worked. He grinned and threw up a hand sign. "Ain't no thing." He finished his coffee in silence then hurried back to work.

He was part of the working community now and, contrary to the indoctrination he'd received in his early criminal days, didn't feel like a chump or a working stiff. No longer a burden or a blight on society as when he was locked up, he felt like a member now of that same society, one who now counted.

He ate half of the delicately cut ham sandwich that Jackie had prepared for him for lunch. Absently, he smiled.

Jackie kept their little place immaculate and never complained, so Roger didn't mind working hard, putting in a lot of overtime. On his off days, though, Jackie made up for all of it. She made him feel like a king. He enjoyed how they sometimes made a palette on the living room floor and played cards. He thought about how much fun they had playing spades, dominoes, and crazy eights. And the lovemaking . . . he had to admit, Jackie had his nose wide open.

He'd just bought Jackie an engagement ring, and they'd planned to get married when they had saved more money. Life couldn't be sweeter.

For a boy who grew up with no chance at life, his life was beginning to look up. He felt like anything was possible.

* * *

The morning L.A. sunshine warmed his back, and his hands felt like he could lift anything. He was young, strong, and virile, and with a good woman at his side, what couldn't he achieve?

He found himself whistling the song from an old *Porgy and Bess* album his mother used to play on their old stereo—before she got hooked on drugs and sold it for a hit.

"I've got plenty of nothing, and nothing is plenty for me."

That morning he was so happy, he just wanted to savor every second. Then he thought about it. He didn't have plenty of nothing, he had a lot of something. Forget the big-willie, big-baller, high-rolling lifestyle of the drug dealers, he was living straight, had a nine-to-five, and was almost off parole. Had a fine woman who was slowly learning to cook, a beautiful baby girl with Afro puff ponytails (she was beginning to take her first steps) and they had their own apartment. What more could a man want?

Roger was lifting a box onto the forklift, awash with contentment and well-being.

"Mr. McKinney, can I see you in my office?"

The words startled Roger so. He craned his neck around to see his boss, Mr. Evans. He felt like he was looking at a ghost.

Mr. Evans averted his gaze.

Roger gulped a wad of spit. "Yes, sir." Right away, he knew something was wrong. His boss had never spoken more than three words to him, and he wasn't even sure he knew his name.

He climbed off the forklift, took off his gloves, and solemnly followed Mr. Evans to the first-floor office.

"I'm sorry, Roger," Mr. Evans told him, "we're going to have to let you go. You didn't report on your application that you'd been arrested five years ago on a drug charge."

The whole time Roger observed how Mr. Evans' razor-thin lips moved up and down. It was as though his ears were stuffed with cotton, yet a roaring raged inside his head. This job had been his second and perhaps last chance.

"But, sir, I paid my debt to society. I'm almost off parole. Haven't I been a good worker?"

"That's why I'm not going to call your parole officer. What you did is called *perjury*."

"I'm sorry."

"You can punch out right now. Come by Friday and pick up your check."

Dumbfounded, Roger couldn't will his feet to move. Clasping and unclasping his fingers, he sat quietly for the longest.

"Mr. McKinney, will we have to escort you out of the building?"

Roger looked up and saw the security guard, Lester Cox hovering over him. He heaved a deep sigh. "No, I'm cool."

That was the longest bus ride Roger ever took home. With each passing block, he dreaded facing Jackie with such bad news. He could see all his hopes and dreams fade, in light of losing his job. How could a day which started out so copacetic wind up so dark?

With each mile he rode on the bus, Roger started feeling more caged, like the cards were stacked against him. *What am I going to do?*

He trudged into their apartment, shoulders slumped inward, mouth turned down at the corners.

Jackie took one look at him and knew something was wrong. "What's wrong, baby?"

Fingers splayed, holding his head in his hands, he told Jackie what had transpired that morning.

Instead of reproaching him for not putting his felony on his application, Jackie was supportive. "Baby, don't worry, I can get a job." She wrapped her arms around his narrow waist and reached up and stroked his long hair.

"No, baby. I want you to stay home with Tamika and take care of her. I'll get another job, don't worry."

"You sure?"

Roger wasn't so sure, but he tried to keep his voice firm and steady. "Don't worry, honey, everything's going to be all right."

Jackie just rubbed his head.

For a while, neither one spoke.

Roger kept his arms wrapped around Jackie's waist, as if he let go he would fall to the floor and bawl like a baby.

As it got closer to the end of the month, Roger still had no job. During the day he kept trying to get a job, this time mentioning his criminal record on the application, but nobody would give him a chance. He'd even gone back to the Job Center. But every job interview they sent him on, he'd discover that either the job had already been taken or the employer didn't want to hire a felon.

More and more he began to drift to the local bar to drink and smoke with his friends at night. Every night he would go to the bar with his buddies, smoke cigarette after cigarette, and slurp down too many beers.

One night he complained to the bartender, "Freddie, ain't nobody tryin' to hire no one out the joint, man. The system is set—They lock a nigger up, and then when he gets out, he can't get or keep a job." He pounded his fist on the bar counter. "I'm a man."

A week later, Roger ran into Termite at the bar. He almost didn't recognize him.

Termite was one of his old playground friends, and used to be his home boy. He now wore his hair in corn-rows and had a huge tattoo of a cobra on his right upper bicep.

Termite approached him first. "Dog, I hear you down on your luck."

"Yeah, dog."

"Well, what you gon' do 'bout it?"

"What you mean?"

"You know . . . you gon' let the system put a foot up your ass again?"

Roger remembered hearing that Termite had done some time in the joint also. "Termite, I ain't 'bout to do no more time."

"You won't, man . . . not if you listen to me."

"What are you talkin' about?"

"Look, dog, I've figured out a way to solve mine and your money problems. I've got it all planned out."

"Okay. What is it, Termite? I'm not saying I'll do it, though."

"You know you my boy and I'm gon' look out for you."

"Hmmm . . . Tell me what it is first."

"Well, you know that check cashing place on Central?"

Roger nodded.

"I've been casing it for four or five months. I just don't have a partner to help me. You want to hear 'bout it?"

"Shoot."

"Okay, dig this. There's an armored truck that picks up the money every Saturday. But Mr. Green takes all the money out the safe on Friday night and has it in bag, waiting to be picked up."

"That sounds too dangerous, Termite. I ain't 'bout to go back to the pen."

"Okay, let's watch the man this Friday, and you'll see what I mean. He do the same *thang* every week, like clockwork."

Roger hesitated, before finally relenting. "Okay."

"L'il nigga, I knew you had heart. You my boy. You know I was gon' look out for you."

The following Friday night, about 8 p.m., the two men huddled in Termite's re-modeled 1964 Thunderbird and watched Mr. Green, the owner of the check cashing place, close his store just before dark.

In South Central L.A., as in many other inner cities, the check cashing place was often where people went to do just what it said—*cash checks*—because, for one reason or another, they didn't have bank accounts, or if they did, couldn't wait for their checks to clear. At an exorbitant fee for such a transaction, the check cashing businesses made what the "project-ites" called *good money*.

After Mr. Green locked up his store, he closed the gate, took a briefcase to his car, and drove off.

As Roger and Termite cased the joint, they did notice that the police drove through on a regular basis. That meant that, to execute their plan, they would have to park their car around the corner on a side street, walk to the store, get the money, and walk back to the car.

Later that night, Roger went home to do some serious thinking about what was about to take place. He really didn't want to go down this route, but he felt like he had no choice. He couldn't get a job, bills were due, and he didn't want to let Jackie and Tammy down. He promised himself that if he participated in the robbery, it would be just to hold him over until he got another job to put him back on track.

He tossed and turned so much that he woke up Jackie in the middle of the night. "Baby, you okay? Stop stressing. Everything's going to work out."

When Jackie took him in her arms, Roger felt as safe as a baby. Usually when she snuggled up to him like that, he would get an erection and make love to her, but his mind was too distracted of late.

Come to think of it, they hadn't made love since he'd lost his job.

Jackie used to be his safe haven. Now the terrible world outdoors had come inside their humble little abode. He'd always known it wasn't a safe world out there—ever since he'd lived in a shelter with his mother—but now it wasn't a safe world inside either.

Now he'd decided he was just going to have to go out there and snatch him a bit of safety for Jackie, his baby, and himself.

Chapter 10

Now it was time to carry out the plan. The night before "the big day," as they called it, Roger and Termite caught the bus to Westwood, stole a Ford and left it parked under the bridge near Watts until it was time to put everything into motion.

"You think the Ford will be safe here?"

Termite nodded. "Sure."

Roger looked at his friend, and it struck him. The way Termite's mouth curled in the corner, he had done this before.

The morning of the robbery, Jackie sensed something was wrong because Roger didn't say much at all. A worried look soured his bronze face. Studying Roger, she removed his plate from the table and noticed his scrambled eggs, oatmeal, and toast were untouched.

With Tamika propped on her hip, Jackie turned to him

and cast a quizzical look. She twisted her mouth to the side and lifted her eyebrow. "What's wrong, baby?"

Tamika began to babble, "Dada, Dada."

"Look, she's saying your name."

"That's daddy's little girl," Roger said, absently, his eyes staring off into space.

"Now why are you looking so crazy?"

"Nothing." Roger's jaw melted into a set, clinched look.

"Didn't you put in some applications this week?"

"Baby, I did, but ain't nobody lookin' to hire nobody fresh out the joint."

Jackie let out a sigh. She put Tamika in her highchair and slid a spoonful of baby applesauce into the baby's mouth.

Over and over, sounding like the pound of a surf, the words roared through Roger's head. *I'm a man, I'm a man, I'm a man.*

As the man of the house, he had to do what he had to do to feed his family. He'd read somewhere that hungry men *will* eat by any means necessary. He had already exhausted his $400 savings, and Jackie was planning to go down to welfare and get food stamps the following week. Today was Friday. He had to stop her, at any cost—*I'm a man, I'm a man, I'm a man.*

Just the thought of his family in the welfare lines made him cringe. Memories of sitting with his mother as a little boy (he couldn't have been more than five) for endless hours at the county office, the white lady peering over her stove-lid spectacles, examining him and his mother like they were the scourge of the earth, while his mother disclosed all of her personal business, burned a hole in his heart.

Oh, no, he didn't want that for Jackie, Tammy or himself. He couldn't see himself being like some men, waiting on what the L.A. residents called "Mother's Day"—the first and the fifteenth of every month—for their girlfriends and baby's moms to get an AFDC check. He didn't want to live off Jackie's check. He loved being the head of the household and taking care of his responsibilities like a man.

Jackie shook her head. After she finished feeding Tammy, she took her out of her highchair, then sat down and ate breakfast in glum silence.

Slobbering, Tammy turned her head from side to side and studied her mother curiously, as if to say, "What's the matter, Mom?"

Earlier, Roger had called Termite from the corner phone booth. There was no turning back now. He took a deep breath. "Jackie, I'm going out looking for work today."

Jackie gave him a strange look, but didn't say anything.

Roger felt worse than if she'd argued with him. She was so trusting. And the truth was, he'd never lied to her before. But he reminded himself, *I'm a man, I'm a man, I'm a man. And a man gotta do what a man gotta do.*

An hour later, Roger met Termite by the car at their assigned meeting place. He looked over his shoulder and panned the area.

A few winos who had slept under the bridge the previous night stared on with dispassionate, glazed eyes. One particularly gaunt old man reached for a brown bag of wine and gulped down the last corner, before throwing the bag on the ground.

Another derelict scrambled to pick up the bottle and drain any that was left down his throat, his Adam's apple moving like a throttle up and down his thin neck.

Roger turned his head away. He didn't want to become like these losers. No, he had to try to fight this fate.

Termite coughed against his fist and cleared his throat. "We're going to wait until closing time, about five o'clock."

Roger nodded.

They spent the day in the park, waiting and going over their plans.

"Now, Termite, you sure we won't get busted? I can't stand to do no mo' time." Roger picked up a ball a young boy had hit and threw it back to the team of young players playing stickball.

"Thanks, man," the young boy called out.

There was something about the little boy's innocence. It reminded Roger of himself when he was growing up. If only he'd never had to grow up to see the world for what it really was.

"Stop trippin', Roger. Just chill. This gonna be a piece of cake."

"I dunno."

A bad feeling stirred in Roger's stomach, but he ignored it. It made him think of his former charge—breaking and entering of a pawn shop—in which he'd been involved six years earlier, when he was seventeen going on eighteen, yet tried as an adult.

"Don't worry, man. Put this on." Termite handed Roger a baseball cap and large sunglasses that covered most of his face. Termite then slipped on his disguise, which matched Roger's. "Pull your hat down closer to your shades."

"Okay. Ready to roll?"

"Let's bounce."

Roger heaved a sigh, shook his head up and down, and started up the car. With Termite riding shotgun, Roger crept down the street, both looking vigilantly about, hoping that the surprise attack would work.

Once there, he parked the Ford around the corner, away from the store, and the two men got out and shambled down the street. They both tugged at the baseball cap over their glasses.

One by one the workers left the check cashing place then got in their cars.

Panning the area, they sat on the bus stop bench and waited for Mr. Green to come out of the store.

Finally, Mr. Green emerged, his silhouette framed in the door.

They watched him set the alarm, his moneybag clutched securely to his side.

Just before he was on his way out, Roger and Termite rushed to the door to catch him.

"Get back in the store," Termite said coldly, the gun pointed into Mr. Green's back. "I have a gun. Disarm that alarm."

Hands trembling, Mr. Green punched numbers into the alarm system and shambled back into the store.

Stepping slowly inside, Termite snatched the bag out of the old man's trembling hands, while Roger pulled the phone out of the wall.

"Please, don't hurt me," Mr. Green pleaded.

"Cooperate and you won't get hurt," Termite said in a muffled voice. "Give me your keys."

What happened after that sped by in a blur for Roger, reminding him of a movie, its film running backwards.

"Get in the bathroom," Roger ordered.

After Mr. Green stumbled in, they locked him up in the bathroom.

"Termite, you didn't tell me they have a TV monitor." Roger cast a wary eye at the camera in the back corner.

"Don't worry about that. That's why we got the disguise."

The two men moved with precision.

Everything went as planned . . . until they headed back and saw two policemen calling up the plates on the car. So then they had to turn back around towards the store.

As they approached the store they saw the owner opening his bathroom door by the combination lock on the inside. They tried to run, but Mr. Green surprised them by running after them.

Before they knew what had happened, Mr. Green went into his truck, got a gun, and started firing.

Roger got hit and didn't even realize it.

He was apprehended by some firemen, who, for no apparent reason, were washing down their truck. When they heard the ruckus, they saw Roger running with the bullet in his leg, and they tackled him. And of course, the police heard the shots and came back to see what was happening.

Looking back, Roger later understood that because of his desperate moves, everything that could go wrong did go wrong. He learned the hard way that you always had to prepare for the unexpected.

* * *

Five miles away, Jackie had just watched the soap operas, "my stories," as she called them, and had put Tammy down for her nap. The main character, Bianca, had just gotten married for the sixth time.

"She's no good, Burt!" Jackie screamed at the TV screen. "Watch that two-timing slut. She'll take you for everything you've got."

Jackie wished she had a phone so she could call her homegirl Lisa and talk about that hoochie mama Bianca from *This Is Your Life.*

After her soaps went off, Jackie started ironing Roger's work shirts, thinking of how happy he had been when he was working. She loved putting the starch on his shirts, which made them look like they had gone to the cleaners. Even though Roger wore the shirts now when he went to the bar, Jackie continued to wash, starch, and iron them anyhow.

It won't be much longer, she thought to herself. *He's a good man. He'll find another job.*

Her eyes scanned the apartment. There was the kitchen table Roger had made for her from a thrown-away table. There was the couch Mom had given her. They had some inexpensive brand-new furniture they were making payments on.

Jackie was a girl of simple pleasures, and it didn't take much to keep her satisfied. But Roger had been unbearable this last month.

Mrs. Smalls told her, "That's how all men are when they are out of work."

Jackie sighed as she tested the iron with her spit on the tip of her finger and resumed ironing. She hoped things would get better. In fact she thought to her self, *Things can only get better.*

At six o'clock, Jackie absently turned the TV on to the news. She went into the kitchen to make a simple dinner of fried chicken, rice, and beans.

A few words caught her attention as the local newscaster previewed an upcoming story—"Robbery . . . local check cashing place . . . suspect shot."

She paid closer attention to the full story:

Two Black male suspects robbed a local check cashing place at gunpoint. One unidentified suspect fled and got away on foot, and the other was apprehended, a Roger McKinnley. He was shot by the owner as he attempted to get away and was taken to a local hospital.

It wasn't unusual for the Los Angeles news to be broadcast shortly after a crime was committed or to televise a pursuit, since they used satellites and helicopters for their news team.

Jackie screamed so loud, when she heard Roger's name, Tammy began to wail. She dashed to the bedroom, grabbed the baby up in her arms, and ran to the local pay phone and called her mother.

Jackie was so distraught that her words couldn't come out clearly. Between ragged breaths, tears, and screams, she was almost unintelligible.

Tamika, who sat squarely on the side of Jackie's slender hips, began to cry too.

"What are you saying, Jackie? What's the matter?" Her mother asked over and over. "Calm down before you upset the baby."

Finally, Jackie was able to string together a coherent sentence so that her mother could get the gist of what she was saying. "They shot Roger. It was on the news."

"Calm down, Jackie. I'll call the police precinct and see if I can get information."

Chapter 11

"Hurry! Roger was taken to the hospital," Wylene said to Annette when she walked into her mother's house from her secretarial job, "her good county job," as they called it.

Jackie, who had run all the way to her mother's house, was pacing back and forth through the living room, tears running down her face.

Annette clutched her purse to her breast, a look of fear washing over her face. "Why? What happened?"

"All we know is Roger was shot." Mrs. Smalls kept her voice calm. "We need to get to County General."

Annette pulled out her car keys. "C'mon, let's go."

Jackie was too numb to talk. She vaguely remembered Yoyo and Leilani taking the baby out of her arms. She'd run so fast, she couldn't even remember how she'd made it to her mother's house.

The neighbors sitting on their porches and the young

men gathering on the corner had sped by her like a film reeling backwards.

In a state of shock, Jackie and Tamika piled into the back seat of the car, while Annette and Mrs. Smalls jumped in the front.

Annette pulled off from the curb, with the gas pedal to the floor.

On the wild drive to the hospital, Jackie kept shaking her head and sighing.

"Don't worry, Jackie." Mrs. Smalls reached in the back seat and patted her hand. "Just wait and see. I'm sure this is a case of mistaken identity."

Jackie didn't say anything. Suddenly, she shuddered. Her toes and fingers felt paralyzed, and blood coursed through her veins like frozen sludge. How could her newly created life be crumbling around her like this? How could Roger do this to her and Tamika . . . just when she and him were building a life together? What was Roger thinking? What had gotten into him?

Mrs. Smalls and Annette waited in the car with Tammy, while Jackie sprinted into the county hospital.

"You sure, you don't want us to go in with you?" her mother asked.

Jackie had calmed down enough to believe that it really wasn't Roger. "No, I'll be all right."

When she got inside the hospital, she went to the information desk. "Roger McKinnley."

The lady at the information desk checked on a computer. "He's on the sixth floor, but he's under police guard and arrest. You can't see him."

Jackie pretended to walk away, but then she turned

back. She rushed up to his floor, but two cops were guarding. She then learned that Roger was not to be allowed visitors that night, or ever. Later, Jackie was relieved to find out that Roger had only been shot in the leg.

The next day, after he was treated, they took him straight to the county jail. The police determined that his injuries weren't serious enough to warrant a continued stay in the hospital.

As much as Jackie hated to see the barren inside of the county jail, hated to smell the industrial strength cleaning smells and the oppressive odors of so many men housed in one place, she hated even more seeing Roger's haunted eyes through the bullet-proof glass.

On her first visit, she had to ask him. "Why, Roger? Just tell me, why'd you do it?"

"I—I—"

"Please tell me something."

"I had no choice, Jackie."

"What do you mean, you had no choice? Did someone put a gun up to your head? Don't tell me you didn't have a choice."

Roger dropped his head into his palms. Finally he looked up at Jackie with spooked eyes. "Jackie, a man does what he has to do to protect his family."

"Do you call this *protecting his family*? You're in jail, Roger."

"Jackie . . . I'm so sorry."

"But why?"

"I'm a man, Jackie, a black man. I had no choice."

"Choice? I don't get it."

"You don't know how it feels to be trapped. I was up against a wall." Roger laced his fingers over his forehead then pulled his head down on the table.

"Trapped? Like I'm living the life, here in the projects. I thought one day we'd buy a little house and get out the projects."

"I know, I know. I'm sorry, Jackie."

"No, you *don't* know. I've never even been outside the projects. You have to draw the line sometimes."

"Jackie, I was desperate. I didn't plan on getting caught."

Jackie just shook her head. Gushes of wind came out the side of her mouth. She didn't know what else to say.

"I don't mean to let you down. Get in touch with Termite. Here's his mother's number. He came to visit me and he said he has my part of the money. He'll give you money each week."

"Can we go ahead and get married?"

"Sure, Jackie. That's the least I could do."

Jackie kissed her pinkie and placed it on the glass separating them. "I'll stick by you."

Before they issued Roger his time, Jackie would visit him every day since the city holding jail was only one bus stop from downtown L.A.

Roger kept his word. Termite would pay Jackie's bills and supply her with grocery money.

The next six months reeled by in a blur. Roger went to trial. Upon the advice of his court-appointed lawyer, he pled guilty and was given twelve years, owing to his prior record.

Meantime, Jackie was to learn a new word now—*recidivism.*

While sentencing, Judge Harvey had droned on about, "Recidivism this . . . recidivism that."

From inside the joint, Roger continued his arrangements for Termite to help pay Jackie's bills and supply her with grocery money.

During this time Roger and Jackie also purchased wedding rings. They got married before he left town to serve his twelve-year prison term, but she still wasn't allowed conjugal visits with him.

For the first year, Termite kept his promise and took care of Jackie, as well as kept money on the books for Roger.

Unfortunately, one morning Roger called Termite's mother's house and found out Termite had been robbed and killed while trying to buy drugs in an abandoned apartment in New York.

That left Jackie with no other option than to move back home with her mother.

Part II

Chapter 12

In spite of the negative circumstances, the Smalls family found something positive in the situation and was happy to have Jackie and Tammy back home. They gave them their own room, and the sisters took turns watching Tammy whenever Jackie had errands to run.

"Tamika makes me feel young again," Mrs. Smalls would say as she spoiled her only grandchild. "She reminds me of when you were a little girl, Jackie. She is so smart and so pretty."

Meantime, Jackie tried to carry on with her life by applying for jobs, seeking state assistance, food stamps, anything that would help out at the house.

After searching for a job for two months, she began to understand how Roger had become so desperate as to commit armed robbery. Every job she applied to wanted a high school diploma. Eventually she went back to night school and was able to get her GED in four months.

As for Roger, Jackie wrote him as much as possible, because she didn't have a ride to see him and couldn't afford to accept phone calls from him, making it difficult to continue their relationship.

As it turned out, they were denied conjugal visits following their marriage. Roger had gotten into a fight with another inmate and was placed in solitary confinement.

Later on, the idea just didn't seem feasible.

Finally, after six months, Jackie found a part-time job at a local school that was within walking distance of her home. She worked two hours a day in the cafeteria and was also granted food stamps every month she had a job. She was also able to get milk for Tammy with vouchers.

Jackie worked in the afternoon and attended a training center, where she learned basic office skills. Annette took on the responsibility of watching Tammy at that time. She even went on flex time at her county job, going into work at 6:00 a.m. and leaving at 2:30 p.m., in order to be able to watch her niece.

In the projects where the Smalls family lived, a maintenance crew worked to keep it fairly clean. One of the guys seemed quite attracted to Jackie. Whenever she would be at the mailbox or the laundry room, Jackie noticed that the young man would go out of his way to strike up a conversation with her.

Jackie had heard of rebound relationships and didn't consider this man as someone she'd be attracted to. She didn't even know his name, but he was like a fly buzzing around her peripheral vision.

She filled her days with work and caring for Tammy, so at first she didn't notice how lonely she was.

One day when Jackie was at her school job, wiping the table in the lunchroom, she looked up and saw another bronze hand wiping the other end of the table.

"Here, let me wipe that for you."

"I've got it." Jackie didn't know how to take the man's advances. This was the same man who would talk to her at the mailbox and the laundry room. She wondered, *What's he doing here?*

"No, let me help. What's your name?"

"Jackie. And yours?"

"Brett. Brett Holloway."

Although Jackie hesitated as she shook his hand, she felt flattered to have a man's attention again. It had been so long, she'd almost forgotten how a man could make you feel womanly.

Even so, she still wasn't attracted to Brett. For one, he was short and stocky and had a rugged look, and she preferred taller guys. And he wasn't nearly as handsome as Roger.

There was one thing, though, that made her decide to talk to him as a friend. She found out he didn't have a prison record. This time, she was going to make sure she didn't get involved with anyone with a record. Brett also came from a two-parent family, the way she'd been raised for most of her life, *and* he had a job.

Chapter 13

Although Jackie insisted that she couldn't be any more than a friend, Brett was persistent in his courting of Jackie. Brett had what the project people called a "golden tongue."

Whenever Jackie wore one of her flamboyant hairstyles, such as a beehive or a French roll, Brett would compliment her. "Jackie, your hairstyle sure is tight."

If she went and bought a new outfit, Brett would say, "Jackie, you're sure looking fly in that outfit."

He would call her every night and ask, "What's a fine young woman doing sitting at home this time of night?"

As time went by, Brett would stop by her job every evening in his souped-up truck and drive her home. One particular evening, Brett opened the car door for her and said, "Hey, Jackie. Give me some love. What's up, girl?" He liked to hug her every time he saw her.

She hugged him back and laughed lightheartedly. "Hi,

Brett. Thanks for picking up Tammy from daycare the other day."

"No problem. Anytime. Hey, how about going to Martha's Kitchen?"

"I don't know, Brett."

"Baby girl, it's just for dinner."

"But I told you I'm a married woman."

"Well . . . where's your man?"

Jackie was silent. After a while, she relented somewhat. "I have to think about it."

That night Jackie discussed it with Annette.

"There's nothing wrong with going out as friends, but make it clear with Roger. Anyhow, it isn't fair for you to do time too, and you still deserve to have a life."

"But I feel like I'm being unfaithful to Roger."

"Jackie, you're a young woman. I never thought I'd say this to you. You really have been loyal to Roger, but I think it's time to get on with your life."

Jackie widened her eyes in mock horror. "I can't believe you, Miss Prude, are saying this."

Annette flipped her hand as if batting away flies. "Jackie, you're not getting any younger. I have someone I'm interested in. I'm tired of looking at your long face. All you do is go to work and take care of Tamika. I'm really surprised at what a good mother you've turned out to be too. Brett seems like a nice enough young man."

In fact, Brett acted like a perfect gentleman, whenever they spent time together, which made Jackie relax more.

She agreed to go to dinner with him, but made it clear that she was still serious about her marriage and her faithfulness to it. She told him, "I just need a friend to talk to, someone to make me laugh, and try to forget about how much time it is going to be before I'm reunited with the man I love. Can you deal with that, Brett?"

"I understand."

Over the next several months, the two became good friends. Brett also included Tammy in their outings to the movies, to skating, and to restaurants. He even began to take Tammy to and from daycare on a daily basis.

Brett also lavished expensive gifts on Jackie, gold chains, rings, gold hoop earrings.

One girl in the projects said, "She thinks she's the shit now, having her man and all. Look at all that gold that Brett is laying on her."

Jackie wanted to turn around and say, "He's not my man, I'm a married woman," but she just threw her head in the air and kept walking down the street.

A year and a half went by before Jackie knew it. She realized her feelings of friendship were beginning to turn romantic.

Brett had been around for all that time, and somehow, they had never crossed that line. But Jackie wanted to. They had only kissed one time, and Jackie was so shocked by the electricity in the kiss, she had to pull away.

She had been celibate for a long time, and had never had conjugal visits with Roger, which, as time went by, she didn't want anyway. Jackie didn't want to admit it even to herself—Her feelings for Roger were fading, and being replaced by her new feelings for Brett. All along she never meant to fall in love with another man. She'd intended to wait for Roger.

Eventually, she decided that before she started a relationship with Brett, she should come clean with Roger, who, ironically, had stopped writing and wasn't responding to any of her letters. Jackie found out that Roger had heard from some guy in jail that she was cheating on him.

"Ready?"

"I'll be right out." Jackie hung up the phone.

When she stepped outside of her mother's project at five in the morning, the amethyst cast of the distant dawn colored the horizon.

This particular Saturday Brett was taking Jackie to visit Roger in prison, a drive that was about fifty-five miles away in the desert. He waited outside in the prison parking lot, while Jackie went in.

As she walked down the long corridor, Jackie felt so depressed that she could hardly lift her feet. Next, she had to stand in one long line to get checked in and make sure she wasn't bringing in anything illegal to the prison.

After about an hour and a half, she made it to the visiting room, where wives, relatives, and inmates sat at tables and chairs, and armed guards watched over the prisoners and their loved ones. When she first saw Roger in the visiting room, Jackie felt some of the old "heart lift" she used to feel. Roger would always be special to her. He was the one who had really shown her love at a time she most needed it.

Even though they were happy to see one another, they both felt awkward. Jackie thought of how different things were between them now. They used to know what the other was thinking without even speaking. They could finish one another's sentences. Now they both had things they needed to get off their chests. The one thing they had always shared was honesty, but neither one seemed to know where to begin.

Roger went first. "As much as I love you, I don't want you to put your life on hold because of the wrong doings I've committed. That is why I have not written you back. It's so hard for a man to tell his wife to continue on with her life."

"Roger, you were the first man I ever loved. I'll never forget you, and no man can ever take your place or fill the spot in my heart," Jackie said, her voice breaking.

Roger stared at her with icy eyes.

Jackie read the disbelief there. "Up until now, I've never cheated on you. I need male companionship, but I wanted to be woman enough and let you know before . . ." Jackie couldn't continue, tears sluicing down her face.

Roger didn't say anything.

Jackie didn't know how to explain to him how things had gotten out of hand and she didn't know which way to go. She swallowed the lump that had formed in her throat.

There were no more words for all the young couple's dashed hopes and dreams. They both had hot tears in their eyes.

Without a word, Roger took his ring off and left, never looking back.

For the longest time, Jackie sat in the waiting room chair, flooded by happier memories, memories of she and Roger playing spades, of picnics on the Pacific Ocean's beach with Tamika lying on a blanket between them, even the memory of the first time they made love and how gentle he'd been then.

Finally, Jackie willed herself to her feet and left the prison for the last time. She climbed back in the car and didn't say a word. Was she making a mistake? Roger had been a good man, but look how things turned out? What kind of man would Brett turn out to be?

When she closed the car door, Brett raised his eyebrow and looked at her as if to say, "And?"

Jackie dropped her head, tears still streaming down her face. She bit her lip and cried silently. She said nothing all the way home, a ride that lasted more than an hour, due to the heavy noon traffic.

When they arrived at her mother's house, Jackie kept her eyes straight ahead and didn't look at Brett. "I think it's best for us not to see each other anymore," she said in a dead tone. She didn't wait for a response. She climbed out of the car, slammed the door, and head hung, walked into the house.

Chapter 14

"She's not here, Brett." Annette cupped the phone with one palm and signaled to Jackie with the other. The two young women stood in the yellow kitchen preparing a dinner of taco, beans, and rice.

Jackie shook her head and slashed her index finger across her throat as if she would kill Annette if she told Brett that she was at home.

After Annette hung up, she stared at Jackie incredulously. "Jackie, why don't you give the man a chance? He really seems to like you. Has he ever tried to get fresh with you?"

"No."

"Well . . . then what's the matter? If it was about sex, I could see it, but he hasn't even tried anything. He must care for you as a person."

"I don't know."

"He's given you jewelry and never asked for sex?"

"No."

"Well, think about it. You're still young. You deserve a right to happiness."

For some reason, Brett wouldn't accept that Jackie didn't have any feelings for him, so he called and called, and kept coming by the house.

Finally he ran into Jackie at her job. "Hey, stranger," he said, helping her with a bag of small cartons of milk she was taking home for Tamika.

"Hey."

Finally, Jackie explained, "I just need time to myself . . . to sort things out."

Brett threw up his palms. "No problem, baby."

"If you care about me, Brett, you'll respect that."

Brett nodded. "I'll be here for you, though."

That same night, when she checked the mail, a letter from Roger had arrived. Jackie opened it and found divorce papers signed by Roger. She let out a sigh of relief. She knew it was for the best, because Roger wasn't doing her any good where he was, and to top it off, twelve years was too long for her to wait.

Shortly after Jackie received the divorce papers, she agreed to go on a picnic with Brett on the Santa Monica pier. Jackie enjoyed all the sights and sounds and side shows at the ocean, the man who tamed snakes, the musician who played seven instruments attached to his body, the fortune-teller, all of it.

When they sat on a blanket, Brett opened his picnic basket and took out a lunch he had prepared. Sensuously, he fed her strawberries dipped in whipped cream. He kissed the whipped cream off her nose. Later, he brushed Jackie's hair, which was now below her shoulders.

He turned out to be as romantic as Roger, and for the first time, Jackie admitted she was falling in love with him. She never thought she'd love again after Roger, but here she was, falling in love again. After all, she was still a young woman, not even twenty years old yet.

Within the next six months, Jackie and Brett became serious and moved around the corner from her mom to a three-bedroom apartment. Within a year, they had a little boy and named him Brett Junior. Jackie was enjoying life with her new love and with her two children.

But down the line, after about their first year together, Jackie noticed that Brett had a number of friends coming to the door at all times of the night.

When he wasn't home (Brett still worked his job as a maintenance man) people in the projects, many of them with an unsavory look, would always ask her, "Where's Brett? Is there any way I can get in contact with him?"

Jackie was getting curious, raising all kinds of questions in her own mind. *Where did all the money come from to buy his truck? How did he get the money to buy me all the gold jewelry he'd given me while we were courting?* One night she broached the subject with him. "Brett, what's going on?—Is there anything I need to know?"

"Don't worry," he replied. "I got this. Let me handle my friends, and you tend to your family around the corner."

Although she'd had a baby at a young age, Jackie was still very naïve and simply didn't possess street sense.

One day while she was at her mother's house sitting with her children, Ross pulled her to the side, a concerned look on his face. "Sis, I have something to tell you."

Jackie's curiosity was piqued. "What?"

Ross spoke in hushed tones. "You know . . . I been meaning to tell you . . . Brett sell drugs on the side. Yes, quite a few people gettin' the little glass dick from him."

Jackie was shocked. "Oh, no! I don't believe it." Jackie was flabbergasted. Like many young women, Jackie saw only what she wanted to see, heard what she wanted to hear, and believed what she wanted to believe. She wanted to believe that her man meant her and her children some good.

"I'm going to talk to him."

Jackie begged, "Please don't say anything."

"Yes, I am, Jackie. I'm going to, before something happens to my niece and nephew. If anything happens to them"—He pounded his fist in his palm—"I'll kill him."

"Promise you won't say anything," Jackie pleaded with Ross. "*I'll* talk to him."

"All right, but you better check that fool."

That same night Jackie confronted Brett about what she'd heard. Before she could fully get the words out of her mouth, Brett grabbed her by the neck and pinned her up against the wall and looked her in the eye.

Stunned, Jackie couldn't believe what was happening. Roger had never hit her, and as nice as Brett had acted at first, she didn't think he'd ever lay his hands on her either.

"Look, Jackie, I was making money before I met you, and I'm not going to stop! Either you live with it or get out, because I'm not going anywhere. One thing I know— You better stop questioning me about what I'm doing."

Brett left that night and didn't come back until the next day, and nothing more was said about it.

Jackie was beginning to feel a little afraid of Brett. What ever happened to the kind, courteous man who had pursued her for a year and a half?

As time went on, Jackie noticed that Brett and Ross had developed a hate for each other. She felt torn since she hadn't had this problem with Roger. Roger loved her family, and the family loved him. Now she was with a man who refused to step inside of her mother's house anymore. She didn't know what to do. She didn't want to leave, because she was pregnant with baby number three, and she didn't want to go back to her family and be a burden again. And somewhere in her heart, she still loved Brett. She just didn't know if he loved her anymore. *He sure doesn't act like it.*

Chapter 15

Ross walked through the projects, a sense of wariness hawking him, which he hadn't felt when he was younger. Groups of street-corner men lounged in front of liquor stores. Danger lurked in every sensuous curve of the young men's sinewy limbs, and the few "O.G.'s" who had survived shootings, prisons, and various addictions sat in wheelchairs or leaned languidly against walls, a toothpick twitching in the corner of their mouths.

Mail was seldom delivered because both the truck and the bags had been stolen at different times. People usually picked up their mail at the welfare office and the post office.

After the drug trade began to develop, Ross, along with all the law-abiding citizens who still lived there, saw a noticeable difference in the projects. Whereas the projects used to be a place of community, now it had become a virtual war zone, right about the time he was approaching adolescence. Funerals of the young became commonplace. In fact, he'd lost several of his schoolmates to gang violence.

It all began at the end of Jackie's eighth month of pregnancy. Brett had a feeling that Ross had told Jackie what was going on. That could have been the only reason she confronted him.

The day of the confrontation Ross stared Brett in the eye as he spoke. "Man, if anything happens to my sister or my niece and nephew because of your slinging rocks, you're going to have to answer to me."

Brett stood toe-to-toe with Ross. "Oh, I'm supposed to be scared or something?"

"This is not a threat. It's a promise." Ross stared Brett down until Brett walked off and climbed into his truck.

After Ross confronted Brett, then Brett knew for a fact why Ross wouldn't speak, call, or come over to his sister's house.

As it turned out, Brett had stopped going over to Jackie's mother's house. He knew how the family felt about him. Mrs. Smalls always stared at him with a strange look, and Annette, Leilani, and Yoyo barely opened their mouths. Everyone acted as if he were invisible and only spoke to his son, Brett, Jr.

At first, the family seemed to welcome him, but Brett knew that things had changed and could only attribute it to Ross telling the family about his extracurricular illegal activities.

As far as Ross was concerned, he understood Jackie's dilemma. She was stuck with that fool but had to try to stick by her man. After all, she was pregnant with baby number three and was due in about a month.

One afternoon while Ross was at work, he decided to talk to his best friend Cornbread about his argument with Brett. It had been several months since he'd spoken to Jackie about Brett's activities. As far as he could see, Brett was still selling drugs, because there were still swarms of traffic going in and out of his house at different times of night.

Though he wasn't worried about Brett being a threat, Ross was still concerned that things seemed a little more strained between him and his sister.

"I think Brett told Jackie what I told him," Ross confided in Cornbread, as the two punched the clock at 2:30 p.m. and got ready to get off work.

"Man, you know Jackie is crazy about you. She still comes around. I didn't see her act any different towards you."

"It's not so much Jackie, but Brett. He doesn't come over to Mom's house anymore. He won't call or speak to anybody. I sure don't trust him. I hate Jackie's having another baby by that fool."

"Ah, forget it. It's probably nothing."

"See you later, man."

"Peace." Cornbread turned at his street corner. (He lived around the corner from Ross's family.) He stopped and turned to face Ross. "Watch your back, brother."

Ross nodded. At nineteen, he was a hard-working young man. Even the local gangbangers respected him, and, from early on he'd never conformed to their demands at thirteen, and they no longer tried to pressure him to join them.

Everyone in the projects said Ross was "good people."
He worked at Wu Tsing's Meat Market during the day and
attended the local junior college three nights a week. He
contributed part of his pay to his mother, and felt like the
man of the house.

Ross still liked to dance, but new dances had replaced
the breakdance. He liked music, but didn't like the new
rap music and the violence and drugs the lyrics seemed to
propagate. Growing up in a houseful of women, he particularly didn't like how they called women *bitches* and *hoes.*
He didn't like seeing some of the girls he had grown up
with selling what was left of their bodies for nothing but a
piece of rock cocaine. (*Base heads* was what the local people called the addicts.)

Later that evening, Ross was walking to his girlfriend
Ashanti's house. Two blocks away, he noticed Shae Shae,
one of the girls he grew up with, walking the larger boulevard in a short mini skirt. He knew she was trying to pick
up a trick, to get some of this new drug called "crack."
She'd lost her hips, her breasts, so he wondered who
would even want to sleep with her. Her hair was matted,
and her clothes dirty and disheveled. No wonder they
called them "strawberries," the women who slept with
men to get crack. He felt bad because he remembered
when many of them had been nice girls and decent citizens. Now, they looked like walking death.

Because of the crack epidemic, Ross, for the first time,
was considering moving out of the projects, the only
home he'd ever known. He shook his head. It saddened
him to see some of the young men and women he knew
scratching, dirty, and disheveled, becoming ghosts of who
they used to be.

He was about seven doors away, when he saw Ashanti's younger sister, Lanette, sitting on the porch and chanting, "Rock steady, 'cause your team ain't ready."

Four girls were playing double dutch in front of her house. Three little boys who looked to be about seven or eight years old were on their knees shooting marbles. It reminded Ross of "the good old days." Although he was only nineteen, he felt older. He'd seen so many of his classmates, particularly the males, get killed. He was tired of going to funerals and, for the first time in his life, no longer felt safe.

That evening, many of the older neighbors were sitting on their porches, catching the evening breeze. Mr. Collier was watering his grass. He and his wife, Miss Corrine, were life-long customers of Wu Tsing's.

"Hello, Mr. Collier."

"Hello, Ross. Thanks for delivering those groceries to my wife."

"You're welcome, sir."

"You're turning out to be a fine young man."

Ross beamed. "Thanks!"

"Hey, Lanette," he called out, suddenly feeling exhilarated, "is Ashanti home?" He waved his hand.

"Yeah, she's waiting on ya," Lanette called back. She shouted through the screen door, "Ashanti, Ross is heere!" her voice piercing the somnolent evening.

Just when Ross was about two houses away from Ashanti's, a low-rider car sped up the street, creating a cacophony of sound. The jarring screech of burning rubber on the asphalt was an indication to Ross that something was about to jump off. He knew these streets too well not to be able to figure that out.

One of the little boys cried out, "Aw, it's gon' be some shit now."

After that, for Ross, it was like watching everything happen in slow motion. For a moment, he didn't know whether to move or to stand still. He froze in his tracks.

Lanette shouted, "Ross, run!"

Her voice sounded as though it were an echo, or as if it was traveling under water.

Two guys jumped out of the low rider antique Cadillac, and young girls and boys darted for cover, dashing into different directions, hiding under cars.

A barrage of gunfire broke out in a staccato rhythm. *Rat-a-tat.*

"What the_" The blast sounded nearby, silencing Ross's speech.

Young and old ran into their houses.

"Run, look out! DUCK!"

Ross' legs locked for a moment, as time froze.

Suddenly two men jumped out and began firing on Ross.

He finally willed his legs to turn and run. Just then, he felt a hot missile hit him in the back.

Neighbors peeked from behind their curtains and blinds and simply looked expressionless, as if all feeling had been drained out of them, like a vampire had drawn all of the blood out of their veins. Reassured none of their loved ones were among the casualties, they inwardly drew sighs of relief. But then they all had one thing in common. They all knew Ross.

Meantime, Ross' life paraded before him, as the blood oozed out his body, draining him of his life force. Like a screen on his tunnel vision, everyone he knew—his sisters, his niece and nephew, Tamika and Brett, Jr., his mother, even his father—flashed before him. In fact, his entire young life flashed before him.

A feeling of regret washed over him. He knew he'd never get to see his new niece or nephew.

The two men ran up to him and took his jewelry and money. Then they shot him once again in the back. Quickly, they turned and ran, and jumped in their old-fashioned Cadillac.

The car, turning on one wheel, sped around the corner in the opposite direction and away from the street. The car moved so quickly, bystanders were prevented from getting a clear view of the occupants, young men wearing ski masks on their faces.

Ross tried to crawl and drag his body over to Ashanti's house, but it was no use. The last thing he remembered was Ashanti pushing through a throng of people and holding his head in her arms as blood bubbled from his mouth.

"Ross, baby, don't die. Hold on, baby. Please don't leave me."

A neighbor across the street heard the shooting and quickly called the police.

The police arrived to see Ross lying in the street in a pool of blood and immediately called for an ambulance at the scene.

A few minutes later, several more police cars arrived, blue lights flashing and sirens blaring, but there was still no arrest. The yellow cordon, indicating there was a death, was put around the scene of the crime, and stony-faced police guarded the scene of the crime, where there was another senseless killing, another home boy lost.

*   *   *

Deep into the afternoon, just when Mrs. Smalls was about to get off work, she heard the sound of gunshots coming from outside the school, but still off in the distance. Today, for some reason, she sat up in the chair. She instantly sensed that something was wrong. She often shuddered upon hearing the loud sirens of ambulances, squad cars, and fire trucks that traveled regularly through the projects.

Usually, she stopped whatever she was doing, called home, and checked on her girls and Ross, he being foremost in her mind as the most endangered of her children, even though he was a good boy.

Yoyo answered the phone. She had stayed home from school to help take care of Tamika, who had a cold and couldn't go to daycare.

"Where's Ross, Yolanda?"

"He's at work, Mom."

Mrs. Smalls let out a sigh of relief and decided to ignore the gnawing feeling in the pit of her stomach that something was wrong.

Once satisfied that her children were okay, she relaxed and continued with her obligations, until the phone began to ring.

Once the ambulance arrived, the neighbors peeked out their doors, looking relieved. After the paramedics put Ross' body on the gurney in the ambulance, Mrs. Collier came out and saw that it was Ross who had been shot. She quickly got on the phone and called the Smalls family. She told them what had happened, as far as she knew, and that she and her husband would drive Mrs. Smalls and her daughters to the hospital.

Mrs. Smalls called Annette, who was at work, and told her what had happened. Annette readily agreed to meet the family at the hospital.

Ashanti climbed into the ambulance and rode it to the hospital, holding Ross' blood-drenched hand.

Once the ambulance arrived, the doctors scrambled in their attempt to revive Ross, but he was pronounced dead on arrival.

Although the news media came out to the scene, the story never made the news. No one wanted to know about a plain, simple, black teen who was neither a gang member nor had any such affiliation, and who was attending community college at the time of his death.

Chapter 16

Although the sun cast bright prisms of light through the stained-glass windows of the church, that Saturday had to be the stormiest day in all of Jackie's twenty-two years. Her mind was a cloud of whirling thoughts. She was oblivious to everyone and everything around her, except for the white casket surrounded by chrysanthemums, which sat five feet away from the front pew. A large placard with a picture of a smiling eighteen-year-old Ross stood beside the casket. It was the last picture had taken of him after he'd graduated from high school. On the wreath was written: "We love you, Ross."

Jackie stared at it, and a long tear rolled down her face.

Her five-year-old daughter Tammy, her sable eyes wide with curiosity, reached up and patted Jackie's face. "Don't cry, Mommy."

When Tammy drew back her plump hand, Jackie noticed how wet it looked. Absently, she took her tissue and wiped Tammy's fingers and smoothed back her daughter's Shirley Temple curls, all in one motion.

"Baby, Mom's all right."

Jackie wished, in fact, that she was all right. She wished this was all a dream she could wake up from and say, "Oh, silly, it was only a bad dream." But she knew this was worse than a nightmare. Despite everything seeming to be shrouded in a gray haze, she knew this was real life and that her baby brother Ross was lying in the casket, never to come home again. Everything felt so unreal, surreal in fact. It reminded her of *The Twilight Zone*, a show that the entire family used to watch on TV.

The church was filled with mourners, from the choir stand, to the pulpit, to the vestibule. There was standing room only, a testimony to Ross' popularity, as well as the Smalls'. Sadness gripped the crowd, as more and more people filed in to pay their last respects. There wasn't a dry eye in the house.

Ross' best friend, Cornbread bit his lip and tried to be manly, as he sat with the family, his face wet with tears.

Suddenly, Jackie heard a long, piercing scream penetrate the solemn air and jumped with a start. She looked back in time to see 14-year-old Leilani flailing her arms, totally out-of-control. Several ushers and the church nurses rushed to her assistance and escorted her out of the church, smelling salts pressed up to her nose.

Several family members and neighbors went to the podium and spoke about Ross' life, but they all broke down, overwhelmed with grief, and were unable to conclude their remarks.

Next, Annette read the obituary. Miraculously, she was

somehow able to remain composed until she read the last words. Then she too broke down in tears.

This was Minister Norton's cue. He stood up from his chair on the dais to deliver the eulogy. "Ross Smalls, born on December 29, 1969, to the union of Eric and Wylene Smalls, departed this world on August 3, 1988. He leaves to mourn his mother, and his sisters, Annette, Jackie, Natasha, Yolanda, and Leilani.

"Ross gave his life to Christ at an early age and was well-loved by both young and old. He never harmed a single soul and, just to clear the record, was never affiliated to any gang. Which brings me to another subject. Young people, let Ross' death not be in vain. Let this be a living eulogy.

"Young people, I want to talk to you today about an epidemic in the black community. I used to be a high-baller, a drug dealer, before the Lord delivered me. But you know what, sometimes others pay for our sins."

"Tell it like it is," Deacon Mosley urged.

"Preach, Rev," a voice from the choir enjoined.

"We are living with the scourge of drugs in our streets. Our young men are killing one another. This is the new style of lynching. In fact the police don't have to kill you anymore. All they got to do is leave you to yourselves and you end up killing one another. I'm speaking out against genocide. What is happening is the killing of two birds with one stone for the white society. They no longer have to lynch us. They let us do the work. Remember, 'Thou shall not kill.' To Ross' friends, I say to you, Please do not try to retaliate. All that does is continue the cycle of violence. Remember, 'Vengeance is mine, saith the Lord.' "

After Minister Norton delivered his sermon, Jackie heard Ross' girlfriend, Ashanti, scream out, "Oh, Ross, baby, I love you!"

Bereft, Jackie could no longer control herself, and fresh sobs escaped from her throat. Placing her hand over her mouth, she tried to hold her cries in, but failed. Even Paxil, which the doctor had prescribed for her, wasn't working. She didn't want to upset her mother or her sisters anymore than they already were. She wanted to be the strong one, the one to hold up, for the other family members.

"Sis, I know this ain't my business, but word on the street is that Brett is slinging rocks." The words seemed to leap from the coffin and fall straight on Jackie's ears. *"He's peddling the glass dick."*

Was this all her fault? After all, she was the one who had hooked up with Brett. Was Ross' death related to his accusations about Brett's drug dealing? *And where is Brett anyway?* Why isn't he at my side at a time like this? The thought made her shudder. *Did Ross know for certain what he was talking about?*

Her dead brother's words returned to her. *"I told Brett nothin' better happen to my niece and nephew."*

The smell of death and chrysanthemums sank into her consciousness. *Ross was only nineteen, way too young to die. He had his whole life in front of him. Why? Why? Why?*

She thought back over the last week. It felt like something out of a horror movie. When Ross was murdered, nobody informed her about what had happened. The family felt like it would've been just too much for her to handle at such a late stage of her pregnancy. The family also decided against telling Brett, but the news traveled through the grapevine and got back to him anyway.

Brett immediately headed home and told Jackie.

She called her family's house, but no one answered the phone. Snatching up her jacket, her hand holding the bottom of her stomach, Jackie told Brett, "Can you watch the children for me? I'm gonna take a walk around the corner to find out what's going on."

When she arrived at the house, she knocked twice and, when no one answered, she let herself in. As she walked in the door, she saw her younger sister Natasha in the living room crying. At that point Jackie felt an overwhelming sense of loss. She knew something was wrong. Deathly wrong. The next thing she knew, she was struggling for oxygen, lost her breath, and passed out.

Natasha, the only other sister at home, pulled herself together and calmed down. She picked up the phone and called 9-1-1. "I have an emergency. My sister is nine months pregnant, and she just passed out. We don't have a car. Please send an ambulance."

The ambulance got there in quick time and rushed Jackie to the hospital, where the doctors ran a lot of tests to make sure she and her unborn baby were all right.

Jackie's blood pressure had shot up so high, the doctors performed an emergency C-section, with only Natasha, her eighteen-year-old sister, by her side.

Meantime, knowing what was going on, Brett couldn't hold out any longer at the house with the children. He decided to take them with him to the hospital. When Brett arrived there, he found out that Ross had died, and that Jackie had delivered a baby boy at 4 a.m.

As for the Smalls, they had to be happy and sad at the

same time. Mrs. Smalls and her daughters stayed with Ross' body at the morgue for a while, to say good-bye. Then they ran down to the maternity ward to be with Jackie. They knew she was going to want to know what was wrong and why Natasha was crying when she came over. At this point, Jackie didn't know what had happened to Ross. She'd passed out even before she got the news.

That afternoon, after she delivered the baby, just as Mrs. Smalls and Annette went in together to see her, Brett came up to the room just to drop the children off with Jackie's family. He ended leaving right away, since Jackie was sleeping peacefully.

As soon as Jackie woke up, though, she asked, "How's Ross doing?" It was as if, intuitively, she knew something was wrong.

Her mother and Annette didn't say a word. They both just broke down and started weeping.

Jackie jumped out of bed, too crazed out of her mind with grief to worry about her stitches from her C-section, and began screaming at the top of her lungs, "I want to see Ross. Where is my brother?" She tried to get out of the room to see Ross.

Security came in and made everyone leave the room, and Mrs. Smalls and Annette took Tammy and Brett, Jr. with them. Immediately, the doctors had Jackie sedated.

The next day, Jackie was a little more relaxed, and the doctors allowed her family to visit. Everyone came back, except Brett. He had called and told Jackie he was at work, and promised that he'd be there later on that afternoon.

Finally, while the family was alone with Jackie, Mrs. Smalls told Jackie what her spirit already knew, and held her in her arms as she cried and cried.

Later, that same afternoon, while Jackie's mom and Annette were visiting her, they both asked her how she felt about naming the baby after Ross?

Jackie said, "I think it's a good idea. I just need to speak with Brett about it first."

As soon as Brett got to the hospital a few hours later and came into the room, everyone got really quiet.

Jackie felt uneasy. *Something's going on that nobody is telling me.*

Mrs. Smalls said, "We'll leave you two alone for a while," and she and Annette left the room.

Moments later, Mrs. Smalls and Annette heard screaming and yelling coming from Jackie's hospital room. They ran in to see what was going on. They got there just in time to see Jackie crying hysterically and Brett leaning over the bed and yelling in her face.

Jackie was screaming over and over, "What do you know about Ross' death, Brett?"

"I don't know what you're talking about!"

Mom tried to step between the arguing couple, before the scene could escalate to an all-out physical fight. "Brett," Mrs. Smalls said, her voice quietly insistent, "please leave, or I'm calling the police." But Brett and Jackie continued to argue.

The staff and other patients must have overheard them, and someone must have called security, because they were there swarming all over the room in no time at all.

Brett grabbed the baby's gifts and threw them on the floor and left, but security caught up with him and escorted him out of the hospital.

After that episode, the hospital staff decided that Jackie could only have one visitor at a time.

"Please keep a close eye on Jackie because she's been waking up two, three times a night," Mom told the hospital staff.

"She keeps breaking down in crying fits," Annette added.

Mrs. Smalls informed Jackie that she was displaying all the symptoms of depression and recommended that she see a psychiatrist, but all Jackie kept saying was, "I'll be okay."

The funeral uppermost in her mind, Jackie was a little concerned that she hadn't seen Brett since the argument at the hospital and that they had talked only once. When she last spoke with him on the phone, she said to him, "I named the baby *Benny Ross* Smalls."

Brett snapped at her. "You gon' put your people before your man? I ain't pickin' you up then. Let your people pick your ass up from the hospital." Brett slammed the phone down in her face.

Jackie was too stunned to speak.

Since she wanted to be with her family for the wake and the funeral, against medical advice she discharged herself from the hospital. Jackie could feel the stitches in her C-section giving her pain, but she just held her stomach. When Brett didn't show up after she'd decided to leave the hospital, she went on and called Annette to come pick her up.

Once Jackie got home from the hospital, since Brett was not coming around, she and her children spent most of their time at her mother's house. For the next two days, the neighbors were bringing in dishes of warm food, but there was nothing they could do to comfort the family.

Jackie thought about her mother slumping to the living room floor at one point. She had to be taken to her room then.

Later, Mrs. Smalls emerged, a sense of calm settling on her face. She announced, "I've prayed and asked God for strength. I have to be strong for the rest of you."

Jackie shook her head and wondered why she was remembering all of this, instead of concentrating on the funeral and saying good-bye to her only brother.

Jackie was so caught up in her thoughts that she didn't hear the commotion in the back of the church. Without warning, pandemonium broke out. People were talking all at once, and a sense of chaos prevailed.

Her stomach quaking, she craned her neck around to see what all the fuss was about. She thought it might be another drive-by shooting. She'd heard of some recent funerals being desecrated by drive-by shootings. She got angry just at the thought. This wasn't the time, nor the place. Oh, no. After all, she'd just lost her baby brother to a senseless shooting. *This couldn't be happening.*

In spite of how numb she felt, what she saw at the back of the church shocked her even more! "What the—" The words stuck in her throat. It was him. Her father! She hadn't seen him, since he'd left home four and a half years earlier.

Dressed in an outdated suit that hung off his gaunt figure, her father, grayer and ashier than Jackie could recall, seemed to have aged more than the four and a half years that she hadn't seen him. He looked like a wisp of the man he used to be.

An eerie silence fell over the church. The stream of mourners seemed to stop, their mouths hanging open, to gawk, and the soloist stopped singing "Precious Lord," the organist's last note echoing throughout the sanctuary.

Mr. Smalls went and sat next to Mrs. Smalls, who just looked at him. He put his arm around her shoulder, to unite them in grief over the loss of their only son.

Finally, Annette, being the take-charge type and eldest in the family, marched to the podium. She cleared her throat and wiped her tears away. "I am glad to see my father here today to show his respects, but we're having a hard enough time as it is dealing with this tragedy. The family is not ready to deal with you being here. You were not here for us while Ross was alive, and we would like for you not to be here now."

Jackie looked on with mixed feelings, as her father stood up, bowed his head, and shuffled out of the church. Mrs. Smalls followed him. A whir of whispers swished through the church like a tornado.

The children all remained seated. They couldn't bring themselves to forgive their father for what he'd done to their mother.

Another hush fell over the church. It was broken by the sound of rap music blasting from a truck. Brett had pulled up in front of the church. Obviously trying to create a scene, Brett had the nerve to be sitting across the street.

Jackie heard one of the doormen ask him to leave. In a gesture of defiance, Brett revved up his truck and skidded off.

After the funeral, the family marched out of the church. Tears gushing down her face, Jackie turned to Mrs. Smalls, as they climbed into the black limousine awaiting the family at the curb. Its final destination was the Inglewood Cemetery, where Ross would be laid to rest. "Mom, how do we move on?"

Mrs. Smalls threw her arms around Jackie. "We live."

Part III

Chapter 17

Six months later . . .

"Brett, where have you been? I'm getting sick of you leaving me for days at a time. What's going on?"

That Sunday morning, Jackie met Brett at their apartment door, ready to do battle. She had her fist balled up. He was going to have to tell her something.

Brett didn't answer. He just pushed past her, came in, went to make a cup of coffee, and sat down.

Jackie walked behind him from room to room, trying to pick a fight, but Brett refused to take the bait. He picked up some more clean clothes and left again.

Since Ross's death, Jackie's relationship with Brett had changed. After that, things were never the same between them anymore.

As days and weeks went by their relationship continued to deteriorate. He would come and stay at the house for two or three days a week, give her some money for the children, and pay the bills for a while, then leave again. Jackie was basically fending for herself.

Once in a while, if she had to, she would serve people drugs from his stash to get the money she needed. She didn't like doing that at all, but she had three children to take care of, and bills to pay.

Annette would fuss at her. "Put him out, Jackie. He's not there for you no way."

Jackie would protest though. "Look, Annette, you don't have any children. A piece of a man is better than none at all. Anyhow, who's going to want me with these three children? I don't think I can make it without Brett's support."

Inside, Jackie began to feel that it was better to have a man around part-time than not have one at all. She also felt that, in time, Brett would come around.

Chapter 18

A couple of years later . . .

Annette, now twenty-four, was dating a young man that she'd met on her job. They'd been dating for a year. Tim was a very bright fellow and had a background in computers, which had landed him a high-paying job with one of the largest companies in the Los Angeles area.

One Friday night he took her out to a posh restaurant called Chez Luis in Beverly Hills. The ambiance in the restaurant was breathtaking. Annette's gaze took in the glistening oak wood floors, the vaulted beamed ceilings, and the spectacular view of the Santa Monica Mountains. Violin music offered a sultry backdrop to a sublime setting.

In spite of the Los Angeles smog, the Hollywood sign loomed in the distance, and colonnades of palm trees swayed in the zephyr.

After Annette gave the maitre d' her order for a lobster,

she was surprised to see two violinists surround her table and play, "Endless Love."

Amazed, Annette looked on as Tim got down on one knee and presented her with a two-and-a-half carat diamond engagement ring.

"Will you marry me, Annette?"

Annette could hardly say anything because she was crying so hard from the sheer excitement.

Tim could barely make out her yes through the mumbles. "What are you saying, Annette?"

So excited, Annette yelled out, "Yes, I will marry you!" She threw her arms around Tim and hugged and kissed him. The on-looking patrons smiled and clapped as they watched the young couple embrace.

Forgetting that Tim had a cell phone, Annette ran to the pay phone to call home and tell everyone her good news.

Over the next six months, the family all pitched in to help plan the June wedding. As Tim, Annette, and her family started making arrangements, Tim and Annette had a slight disagreement regarding whether or not her father should give her away.

Annette didn't want him to, but Tim thought he should.

"Regardless of what your father has done, he is still your dad. This will be one of the most special days of your life."

Annette thought about it. *Didn't we stick by Jackie, all through her ups and down? A family was for good times as well as for bad times.* "You're right, Tim."

"That's my Annette. This is why I love you—You're so caring and have been such a support to your mother and family. I want a woman who I know will be there for me when the going gets tough."

After that speech Annette agreed and sent her dad a letter. She would have called him, but she only had an address for him. When he'd first left, Mr. Smalls always sent letters and money with a return address, but no phone number.

When Annette's father received the letter, he had tears of happiness in his eyes. He had to shake his head at the ironies of life. Sadly, he'd just received the diagnosis from his doctor that he had cancer of the liver and only had about four months to live. He'd planned to just keep this to himself and die alone because he didn't think his children or anyone else cared.

Days before the wedding Tim and Annette moved into their new house, way out in the suburbs in Duarte, away from drug dealers on the corner, drive-by shootings, and random acts of violence.

The day of the wedding everything turned out beautifully. The church was filled with calla lilies, baby's breath, and orchids. Jackie and her sisters were the bridesmaids, and wore soft lavender organdy dresses. Tamika was the flower girl. Wearing a floor-length, lacy dress, she was the picture of angelic innocence as she dropped petals down the aisle.

Tim had enough groomsmen to march each of the four sisters down the aisle. They wore white tuxedos with lavender cummerbunds.

When Mr. Smalls walked Annette down the aisle, Annette appeared very happy to see her father. She wore a designer gown attached to a detailed train with pearls sewn on it.

Everyone said, "Annette is the most lovely bride I've ever seen."

This was the first happy celebration the Smalls had had since Ross' death, and everyone each member of the family knew from the projects, from their schools, and from their jobs showed up.

After the wedding ceremony, everyone had a great time at the reception, which was held in the church's basement. For once, no one cut up, got into fights or arguments, or got drunk. Mrs. Smalls was partly responsible for this because she refused to allow any alcohol at the reception.

The young and old danced together. Everyone formed a long line and did a new dance called the electric slide.

The white cake, topped by a black bride and groom, had lavender roses surrounding it, and a waterfall in the center of its four tiers. The punch wasn't spiked, and flowed through an ice sculpture in the shaped of a dove.

Although they hadn't been close for a long time, Mrs. Smalls could tell something was wrong with her estranged husband, when she saw him at the wedding. Even though he was smiling and laughing, she could still sense something wasn't quite right with him.

Once the introductions of the wedding party were over, no one could find Mr. Smalls. He'd left the reception and went back to his hotel room without telling anyone. Before leaving, though, he'd pulled out an envelope, put one hundred dollars in it, and wrote, "Good luck with your new husband." As an afterthought, he also wrote: "You have made my day by giving me the opportunity to be in your life on your special day. You have given me life and love before death. I have come to my last days, but through you, I carry on. Love, Father."

At the last moment, Mr. Smalls decided to take his card to the hotel with him and not leave it with the mountain of other gifts. He wanted to make sure Annette received her gift.

Around five the next morning, Mr. Smalls packed his things in the van, checked out of the hotel, and got on the road. He was headed back for North Carolina. He made a quick stop at Mrs. Smalls' house, where everyone, except Tim and Annette, had stayed the previous night, and slid a card under the door.

Around 9 a.m., when Mrs. Smalls awoke, she went to the kitchen to start breakfast. While putting on the coffee pot, she noticed the note sticking out from under the door. She picked it up and recognized the handwriting as that of her estranged husband. She took a closer look and saw that it was addressed to Annette, so she called her to get permission to open it.

As soon as mother and daughter read the card, they knew they had to find him. By some stroke of luck, Mr. Smalls had left a phone number, and so they started trying to reach him every hour on the hour.

Finally, later that afternoon, they got in touch with him. Mrs. Smalls questioned him about the meaning of the note. "Eric, what exactly are you trying to say?"

"The doctors say I only have a few months to live, Wylene. I have liver cancer. I don't know how long it will be before—" Mr. Smalls, his voice cracking, was unable to continue.

Mrs. Smalls was silent for a long time, before she finally spoke up. "I knew something was wrong. Is there anything

I can do for you?" Mrs. Smalls was sincere, when she made this offer. If she was a bitter woman, she wouldn't have cared and would have rejoiced in Mr. Smalls' illness, or felt like it was payback for abandoning her with six children to finish raising in the projects. But deep in her heart, she still loved him, as the father of her children. She knew that everyone made mistakes.

She remembered them back when they were teenagers growing up in Shreveport, Louisiana. He'd been her first love, and he'd also be her last.

"No, Wylene. You raised some fine children for me. I can't ask for much more."

After Mrs. Smalls hung up, she called Annette.

In turn, Annette called her father. "Are you on medication?" she asked.

"Yes, but I don't like the way the meds make me feel, so I stopped taking them."

Annette and Tim had planned to fly to Hawaii for their honeymoon, but they decided to cancel the trip. Instead, they had Mr. Smalls come to live with them and had all of his belongings placed in storage. Instinctively, they knew it was just a matter of time.

During the fifth week with them, his health began to deteriorate quickly. The prognosis for recovery didn't seem hopeful at all. That's when Annette decided she wanted to take her father to the hospital.

Mr. Smalls objected though. "No, I want to die with family, not in some old, cold hospital. And besides there is nothing else that the doctors can do for me."

By the end of the week, Annette called her mother and told her that her father had taken a turn for the worse.

She even asked that all the family members come to her house to be with him during his transition. That night, the whole family stayed by Mr. Smalls' side in a prayer vigil.

Mrs. Smalls read from the 23rd Psalm, which seemed to comfort Mr. Smalls. She held his hand and talked to him in low, soothing tones. "Yea, though I walk through the valley of the shadow of death, I will fear no evil."

The way he had the death rattle in his chest, they knew that by the next morning, it would be all over. It was getting harder for Mr. Smalls to hold his eyes open, and you had to put your ear to his mouth to understand what he was trying to say.

Mr. Smalls took his last breath at 5:57 a.m. It was all over. Everyone began to pray and to cry together. Family members were all standing around his bed, holding his hands, or touching some part of his emaciated body.

Jackie was the only one who wanted to be alone. She went out of the room and locked herself in the bathroom, where she screamed through the door, "I'm not coming out until the ambulance gets here and removes his body."

Nobody could fathom why Jackie was reacting that way. Nobody, but Jackie. See, when Jackie was little, she was put on punishment by her father more than any of the others. She would always say how she hated him so much and wished he would leave. Now Jackie felt saddled with guilt for wishing bad on her father all those years ago.

Her family was wondering if her reaction had something to do with the way she was reminded of Ross, when she saw him lying there dead.

Later on that day, everyone stayed together at Annette's house. Her Spanish-style house was a three-bedroom ranch, with a large family room, a Jacuzzi in the back yard, and a beautiful view of the purple-cast San Gabriel Mountains.

Her neighbors were all white and Hispanic and very friendly. Some even brought food over, when they heard Annette's father had passed.

The family spent the day together. They talked over breakfast, played cards, and watched television all day. That evening, they had a large dinner, consisting of gumbo, corn muffins, and rice. Later on that evening, everyone decided, once again, to stay the night; everyone just wanted to be together.

Mr. Smalls was given a simple funeral at the funeral home, and was buried next to Ross.

Over the next few days, the Smalls family tried to go on with their lives by going home and resuming their normal activities.

Chapter 19

A few days after her father had passed, Jackie was back at home in the projects with her children. Her girlfriend Lisa, whom she had grown up with, dropped by. Jackie and Lisa had been classmates in high school before Jackie got pregnant and dropped out of school. In fact, Lisa was the friend who'd given Annette a ride home that first night that Jackie had had sex with Kenny.

The truth was, Jackie really needed time to herself to sort out her feelings about her father's death, but, at the same time, she felt so uncomfortable with her feelings of guilt and remorse that she was glad to have some company. This wasn't the first time she'd felt so devastated. In fact, ever since Ross' death, she'd felt lost.

As it turned out, Lisa was also a customer of Brett's, which was how the two women had really hooked back up as adults. Whenever Brett was at home, Lisa would come by the house to buy drugs, and when he wasn't, Jackie would sometimes serve her.

Lisa said, "I wonder if, now that Brett has gotten married, things will still be the same?"

Stunned, Jackie was quiet for a moment.

"Who did you hear that from?"

"I heard it from the horse's mouth—from Debbie—Brett's new wife. In fact, Debbie's mother showed the pictures of their honeymoon in Tahiti, where they got married, to my mother."

Dumbfounded, Jackie had to sit down, the wind knocked completely out of her. She felt as though someone had socked her right in the stomach.

After Lisa got her drugs, Jackie ran to the phone and paged Brett 9-1-1. As soon as he called back, she cut straight to the chase. "Is it true that you've gotten married?"

Initially, Brett was very quiet.

"Brett, are you there?"

Finally his voice came on line. "Can we talk about this later?"

"No. When were you planning on telling me?"

"I will be right over so we can discuss this."

Jackie paused for a second. She had just slept with Brett the week before, and he hadn't been home since that time, something that had become the norm for him.

Jackie then commenced to going off at the top of her lungs. "If you come anywhere near me, my children, or my house, I will call the police, give them your name and your drugs, and press charges for harassment." Jackie slammed the phone down and started knocking things over, throwing Brett's pictures against the wall.

Lisa rushed out of the bathroom, where she was probably getting high, then grabbed Jackie and shook her shoulders. "Girl, get yourself together. You can't let your children see you behaving like this."

As Jackie calmed down, Lisa added, "Let's go outside and get some air."

As soon as Lisa suggested that, the children came running downstairs to see what was going on. "Mama, what's wrong?" Tamika asked.

At nine years old, Tamika was very mature for her age. Already she could cook, wash, and take care of her younger brothers. When her mother and Brett had gotten together, she was a little over two, but in the seven years since her mother had been with Brett, she'd become like a mother to Jackie's two younger sons. When her Uncle Ross had died and she was only four, Tamika was the one to comfort Jackie and get the bottle for her new baby brother, Benny.

"I'm okay," Jackie told her.

Jackie turned to Tamika, Brett, and Benny and told them to get dressed.

"We goin' some place, Mama?" Tamika asked.

"Yeah, you're going to your grandmother's."

Jackie took a moment to get her composure. She knew that if she went to her mother's house all upset, Mrs. Smalls was going to ask her a million questions.

After they dropped the children off, the two women decided to go to the Oasis, a neighborhood bar, to have a few drinks. Jackie didn't want to stay long because she didn't want to be around a lot of people. She wanted to be some place where she could be private.

"Let's go to my house," Lisa suggested.

Still dazed, Jackie nodded as though she was in a trance.

When they got to Lisa's place, her ten-year-old son, Kris, was sitting outside.

"Kris, be in by 10 o'clock tonight, you hear?" Lisa said absently, as though she could care less.

As soon as they got in the house, they started talking about what had happened.

Jackie broke down and started crying. "That low-life sonofabitch."

Lisa patted Jackie's back. "Girl, don't worry about it."

Without saying another word, Lisa went into the kitchen and pulled two beers out of the refrigerator. She passed one to Jackie then proceeded to the bathroom to get some tissue. She returned with a pile of coke rolled up in a dollar bill, along with a straw and the tissue.

She gave the tissue to Jackie and then opened the bill and started sniffing the coke through the straw. "Why don't you try some of this?" Lisa beckoned Jackie, who was sitting on the loveseat, to come over and try the drug. "It will relax you a little bit, since you had such a hard stressful day."

At first, Jackie hesitated. She'd never used drugs and was only a social drinker. But the thought of Brett marrying another woman after she had borne him two sons was a bit too much to handle. Even Roger had married her, and she didn't even have any kids for him. *The nerve of that rat!*

She shrugged her shoulders then gave in. *What the heck,* she thought. She'd try a little bit. Maybe it would take the edge off some of her pain. To think she had allowed that man in and out of her bed for the past seven years, and then he up and married someone else on her.

Yes, a little coke would help me get through this night. I won't use it again after tonight.

After sniffing the coke up her nose, Jackie looked up and said, "I still feel the same."

So she tried a little more of the white powder, and then a little more.

A few hours passed before Jackie knew it. In fact, time seemed to have taken on a new dimension. On the one hand everything seemed slower, yet on the other, it seemed to be speeding up.

Finally, Jackie said, "I feel more relaxed now, more than I have in a long time."

At 10:10 p.m., Lisa's son, Kris, walked in the living room from wherever he'd been outdoors and startled Jackie, who tried to hide the coke under her shoe.

Lisa glanced over at her. "You don't have to do that. Kris already knows what's up. As long as I don't catch him doing it, we have an okay relationship. He knows that I am grown, and that he is not to do what I do." Lisa gave a snort. "Besides that, you spilled most of it anyway."

Feeling lightheaded, Jackie looked at her. "Oh, but there's more where that came from. Let's go to my place."

Lisa yelled upstairs to tell her son that she was leaving, and that he could not go back out tonight. "If I call here and you don't answer, I will come home and beat your ass!"

They drove back to Jackie's house, and Jackie went and got Brett's stash, something she'd never done before.

The two women started getting high again.

Before Jackie knew it, it was morning. They had gotten high all night long. They didn't even hear the phone ring, although there'd been two calls.

Lisa just happened to look at the clock. "Oh shit! It's 6:25 a.m., and I have to go to work for 9."

Jackie stopped her. "Before you run up out of here, can you hold this bundle for me? Normally I wouldn't ask, but I know Brett still has a key and it's going to take about three to four days to get my locks changed, and I know he will try to take it."

Jackie offered to pay Lisa a couple of dollars, or she could help herself to a couple of bags.

About three days later, after the maintenance man came and changed the locks, Jackie decided that it would be a good time to go over to Lisa's and pick up her package.

When she got there no one was home, so she decided to go pick her children up from school, and then try back later on.

This time when she got there, she saw Kris sitting outside on the porch. "Where's your mom?"

"If she's not here, I don't know where she is, because she didn't have to work today."

"Okay. Tell her that I stopped by."

Jackie went back home. She and the children then went over to her mother's house to have dinner, and have her sister help the children with their homework.

When they were all done, Jackie got the children together, and they went home. As soon as they got in the house she told the children to go get in the tub and then get themselves together for bed.

Just as she was putting the youngest in the tub, she heard someone banging on the door. When she finally got downstairs, she called out, "Who is it?"

Brett yelled back through the door, "It's me."

"What do you want?"

"I came to get my stuff."

Jackie paused. Then she shouted back through the door, "You are not getting anything out of here, unless you come back with the police to assist you."

There was silence.

"Fine, if that's how you want it. Just make sure you don't ask me for nothing . . . not even for the children. If I decide to do anything, it will be because *I* want to, not because you asked." Brett kicked the door and left.

The only reason he decided not to retaliate against Jackie was because she was his babies' mama. At any rate, he knew people always felt that he had something to do with Ross' death and didn't want any more guilt on his conscience.

About fifteen minutes later Jackie heard another knock on the door. She didn't even ask who it was. She yelled out, "You wait right there while I call the police."

She picked up the phone and dialed 9-1-1. As soon as the operator answered, Jackie proceeded to tell her that her ex-boyfriend was banging on her door and demanding to be let in. She told them she felt that he was a danger and a threat to her.

As she stood by the window talking to the operator, all of a sudden Jackie noticed that it was Kris at the door and not Brett. She tried to cancel the call, but they said they had to send an officer over anyway.

Jackie let Kris in the house and told him to come upstairs. He was carrying a big box that looked like a sneaker box. When he got upstairs, he gave it to her.

She opened the box and saw the drugs with a note attached. The note was from Lisa. She explained that some of the drugs were missing and that she had questioned her boyfriend and her son and that they had both said that they didn't even know the drugs were in the house. She also explained in the note that she had used more than she thought, but not all of what was missing. She said she would try to pay for some of it, and that she was really sorry.

Jackie shook her head in disgust. She knew that every little bit counted. That made her even more upset, because she had planned to sell the stuff and use the money for herself and the children. Jackie knew what she had was worth about $5,000, and now what she had gotten back from Lisa was worth only about $1600. She quickly hid the box, when she heard an officer coming up the stairs to her house.

When Jackie opened the door, the officer, a burly black brother, whose badge identified him as Shawn Martin, said, "Yeah, we got an emergency call from this location. Is everything all right in there?"

Jackie nodded. "Oh, I am okay now."

"Fine, but if I have to come back out again, I will have to ask you for some information."

"Okay. Thank you for coming out to check anyway." She closed the door and drew a sigh of relief.

She ran upstairs to make sure that the children were asleep. Then she went downstairs to check out the package Lisa had sent. She opened one of the packets and started to sniff it.

Chapter 20

Seven years later . . .

Jackie was still dealing with child support and trying to get Brett to take care of his children, so she took him to court.

When Brett received a letter in the mail ordering him and Debbie to appear in court, he became irate.

He called Jackie immediately to curse her out. "Why did you have to involve my wife?"

"Later for you, Brett. What do you think your sons are living on? Air?"

After Brett calmed down a little, he offered to make a deal with her in the hopes that she would drop the court order.

Jackie angrily replied, "You want me to make a deal with you and drop the court order? You've got some nerve. You haven't even brought them a pair of sneakers or called just to see how they were doing all of these years! I will see you in court!"

Child support authorities found out that Brett, no longer working, had listed everything he owned in Debbie's name. They also found out that he was also receiving income from rents that he was collecting on several multi-family homes that he owned, not to mention that he also owned a beauty salon, a car wash, and several other lucrative businesses. To add insult to injury, his wife still maintained a full-time job.

The child support agency decided to attach Debbie's paycheck. She would no longer be able to receive her income tax refund, until Brett caught up with the large amount of arrears that he still owed Jackie for their two sons.

Meanwhile, the Smalls family was having a major problem with Jackie and her lifestyle. She was now hanging out in clubs four and five nights a week. Her sisters had heard that she had started to use drugs, and was becoming more than what they considered a social drinker.

But somehow, Jackie still managed to get to work at the county every morning and keep her receptionist job. She'd begun working full-time as a receptionist a year before she took Brett to court.

The irony was that when Jackie was younger she acted older. She'd been a responsible mother, a clean housekeeper, and a good mate. Now, though, it seemed she was trying to make up for her missed freedom and go back to being a teenager.

She hadn't had a serious relationship since Brett, so she

just liked to hang out and enjoy the single life. Most of her dates now had become one-night stands. Her only strong point now was that she never brought the men home to sleep at her house.

She was also beginning to neglect her children in ways that disturbed the family. She didn't give the kids good hot meals, nor did she do their laundry. And her house-keeping standards had gone down. Her thinking was that Tamika, who had just turned sixteen, was responsible enough to handle it for herself and the rest of the children.

Because Jackie wasn't home a lot at night and week-ends, she would tell Tammy what time all three had to be in and would leave her in charge, while she went out for a couple of hours. Sometimes it would be all night.

If there were any problems, Tammy was to call her grandmother or her Aunt Annette's house.

Trying to let her children raise themselves alone was not working out too well. After a while, Brett Jr., now age 14, wasn't listening to Tamika.

"You're not my mother," he would always tell her. "I don't have to listen to you." He never observed his curfew and was defiant any time Jackie or Tamika asked him to do a chore around the house.

Tammy would call her grandmother's house. Then one of the younger aunts, usually Leilani or Yoyo, would end up having to come over and get the children out of the house.

When Jackie would finally show up, sometimes two days later, to collect the children, the whole family would end up arguing with her about the situation. In turn, Jackie wouldn't speak to the family for a couple of days or weeks, before breaking the deadlock. Then the cycle would repeat itself all over again.

The family decided to intervene, to get together to discuss amongst themselves a solution to help with Jackie. They realized that they needed a different approach because arguing with her wasn't working out. They decided that Tammy should stay with Annette and Tim.

Annette didn't think this was a good idea. All Tim ever talked about was having children of his own. Although they had been married over seven years, Tim didn't feel like they were married long enough to be caring for someone else's children, especially a teenager.

Instead of going to her Aunt Annette's home, Tammy wound up staying with her grandmother. Mrs. Smalls couldn't really afford to keep Tamika, but she had no choice because, while Jackie was running the streets, different boys were hanging around the house.

Tamika was a good girl, but the lack of supervision worried her grandmother. Mrs. Smalls knew that Tammy was at that age when girls were ending up pregnant and dropping out of school and get on public assistance. And no one wanted that to happen. They didn't want to see history repeat itself.

Mrs. Smalls sat down and explained the situation to Jackie. "Do you want her to wind up pregnant at sixteen like you did, Jackie?" she asked.

"No, Mom. You're right."

Jackie definitely didn't want her daughter's life to end up like hers. She knew her life was a mess, but she didn't know how to get off the roller coaster. It was as if she'd gotten started on this downward spiral and couldn't help herself. She just couldn't stop her destructive behavior.

Mrs. Smalls wasn't done with Jackie yet. "Jackie, you know this is the age where boys can get in trouble with the law. You don't want what happened to Ross to happen to Brett, do you?"

Mrs. Smalls didn't have to remind Jackie about Brett's defiance with authority figures and his acting out in school.

"You know Ross never gave me a day of trouble and you see what happened to him. We live in too rough a time for you to be leaving your sons alone. You just have to spend more time with these children. You know you're never gonna forgive yourself if anything happens to them."

"That boy is just hardheaded, Mom. I'm doing the best I can."

"Well, can you at least give me forty a week to help with food for Tammy?"

"No!" Jackie huffed. "It was your idea to keep her in the first place. Why should I have to pay you? After all, she is your granddaughter." Jackie then stalked away.

Mrs. Smalls knew, no matter what, she had a responsibility to Tammy, and that Jackie needed some help.

Brett and his wife Debbie arrived at court on time to meet with their retained legal counsel, Attorney Watkins.

Jackie, her clothes wrinkled and disheveled and her hair unkempt, arrived late. Jackie's public defender, Attorney Leighton, let the prosecutor know they could call up their case.

When they went in front of Judge Marjorie Adams, she granted Jackie $750 a month plus $50 more on the arrears, effective immediately, to bring the total to $800 a month.

Of course, Brett's lawyer tried to argue it down, but he couldn't get past the tough, no-nonsense judge.

Unfortunately, even with Jackie receiving more income, she still wasn't keeping up with her bills. Her utilities were getting shut-off notices, and there was never enough food in her refrigerator. Furthermore, she still refused to give her mother any money to help with Tammy or the boys, even though her sons still went to their grandmother's house for meals. Sometimes the boys would go next door to their grandmother's neighbor, Mr. Kelly, to get a hair-cut, but Jackie rarely paid him.

Then the inevitable happened. With her poor work habits and tardiness, naturally Jackie lost her secretarial job with the county.

As time went on, Jackie didn't just disappear at night, but during the middle of the day also. When Benny and Brett Jr. would come in from school, their mother would be nowhere to be found, and they would have to leave the door unlocked to get back in, whenever they went out to play.

Late one afternoon, Kris talked Brett Jr. into taking some money from the corner store up the street, where there was just one foreign lady working by herself.

Kris lured the woman over to the other side of the store to distract her, while Brett hid behind the counter so he could get in the register.

Brett tried to open the register but couldn't. Looking around, he found a bank bag filled with one-dollar bills and shoved it in his crotch.

The two then slipped out of the store without incident. Since Kris was the older of the two boys, he divided the money between the both of them.

The owners had checked the security camera hen they realized that their bag with one-dollar bills was nowhere to be found. That's when they saw Brett and Kris in the act. The owners had no problem identifying Kris and Brett as neighborhood kids who frequented their store. They were picked up later in an apartment in the projects.

After they were arrested, they were both taken downtown to Juvenile Detention.

The counselor's first priority for the newcomers was to contact their parents. After Kris gave his full name, the authorities discovered that the store robbery wasn't his first offense.

The counselor then said to Brett, "What's your home phone number?"

Brett responded, "Our phone is disconnected, and I don't know my father's phone number."

"Is there anyone else I could contact?"

"No."

"Do your parents know each other?"

"Yes, sir."

"Then I'm going to have Kris' mom get in touch with your mother." The counselor tried to get Kris' mother on the phone, but when no one picked up, he just left a message.

When Lisa finally got home from work at about 5:30 p.m., the guys on the block told her what had happened with Kris and Brett.

She took the news calmly. "Thanks for letting me know.

I appreciate your concern." Lisa had been through this with Kris before and knew not to rush down there because he couldn't get out until he was processed and had seen the judge.

When she got upstairs, she saw she had a couple of messages on the answering machine. She listened to them and found out exactly where the boys were. She also knew where to find Jackie.

Lisa felt somewhat responsible and a little guilty about the fact that she was the one to introduce Jackie to drugs. But then she shrugged it off.

Lisa would only go so far and managed to keep up her appearance and her job. She'd heard Jackie had been fired from her job for getting high and missing too much work. And Jackie didn't keep herself neat and clean like she used to. *It's not my fault that she doesn't know how to handle her business.*

Lisa knew exactly where to find Jackie. She drove over to a little hole-in-the-wall club called the Oasis, where the drug dealers sold their product, and the users came to drink, get high, and just socialize. She found Jackie seated between two men and flirting.

Jackie tossed down her drink and threw back her head in raucous laughter.

When Lisa told her about the boys, Jackie panicked. "My baby is arrested?" she said, her voice slurring.

Since Jackie was reeking of alcohol, Lisa took her home to get herself together, so that she could be prepared for any questions that the authorities would be sure to ask.

Later, when they arrived at the center, Mr. Young, the counselor, took each one separately, to talk to them in private.

"Ms. Smalls, where were you in the afternoon?" Mr. Young asked her.

Jackie kept a straight face. Since she'd been fired from her county job, she seemed to lose all interest in finding another job. "I was out looking for another job."

He asked, "So who's in charge of Brett?"

"My sister Natasha Smalls is. Why?"

"Okay. Then we'll release him to you now, but you have to bring him, as well as your sister, to court tomorrow morning to verify this."

Kris was detained since he had a prior record.

After the session with Mr. Young, Jackie was hoping that Lisa would be able to take them home, since she had to pick up Benny from her mother's house.

Lisa agreed to drop Jackie and Brett Jr. off at Mrs. Smalls'. When they stepped out the car, she told them, "Be ready in the morning at ten-thirty. Court starts at eleven sharp."

For the first time, Jackie was worried. She would have to explain to Natasha why she had to go to court with them. It wasn't going to be easy to explain, since the family had been trying to convince her to stop leaving the kids home alone in the first place.

When Jackie walked in her mother's house, everyone was glaring at her with I-told-you-so eyes. She thought to herself, *It seems like they already got the news.*

Arms crossed, Benny and Brett sat and looked on sullenly. Jackie could see the disapproval and hatred in both her sons' eyes.

All of a sudden it hit her. She was the only screw-up in the family, the black sheep. Realizing how low she'd sunk, she felt awful inside.

Yoyo and Leilani, now 27 and 25, were upstanding fine

young women in the community. They both attended college and worked part-time. Natasha, age 29, had finished college and was working as a nurse at a county hospital.

Lord, I want to do right, but these drugs are so powerful.

It was as if the drugs kept calling her from the streets. When she was high, she felt desirable to men, loving and loved. She didn't even feel like she was raising three children by herself. How did her mother ever raise the six of them after her father ran off?

"Can I speak to you in private?" Jackie said to Tasha.

Tasha shook her head from left to right. "Whatever you have to say to me, I think everyone deserves to hear it."

At that moment Jackie broke down and cried.

How did her life become such a mess? When did it begin to unravel? How come Roger had to go to jail and she wound up with Brett, who indirectly introduced her to drugs? His money laundered now, Brett was a "respectable" member of society, and ironically, here she was, the alcoholic and drug addict.

"I'll try to change. Please don't give up on me. Tasha, if you don't come with me to court, I have a good chance of losing all my children."

Tasha's face hardened. "What do I have to go for?"

Jackie started to cry even harder. Between sobs, she explained to Natasha, "I told the people at lockup that Brett was in your care when he committed this crime."

"No, Jackie. I'm not gonna lie for you. It could be even worse. I could be put in jail for perjury, if I lie for you."

Miffed, Jackie took the boys home. She spent all evening going next door to use the neighbor's phone, begging her mother and sisters to forgive her.

During the night the Smalls discussed Jackie's predicament. They decided that no way would they play a part in the court taking the children away from Jackie. Even Tasha herself admitted, "I'll never be able to forgive myself, if I didn't do everything in my power to get those children out of that situation."

So Yolanda went to watch Benny and Brett, while Jackie went to talk to her mother.

"Jackie," Mrs. Smalls began, "we're going to help you, but this is your last chance with us. Even mothers get tired. You've been in trouble for too long."

Jackie began to smile.

"Don't get so happy, missy. Here's the deal—Tasha will go to court with you tomorrow on one condition."

Jackie's smile evaporated. "What is it?"

"You have to sign yourself into a drug treatment program."

Jackie's smile returned. She was ready to do almost anything to get out of this situation. "Okay, I'll do it."

Chapter 21

In court the following day, as both Lisa and Kris stood before Judge Robinson, he reminded Kris, "Young man, weren't you in my court a few months back on drug charges?" The judge started shuffling papers on his desk, like he was looking for something.

Lisa said, "Yes, Your Hon—"

Judge Robinson banged his gavel. "Allow the young man to speak for himself. I asked him a simple question, but already you're running to his rescue. You see, this is the problem with you parents. You never allow the kids to be accountable, and in the end, you end up with a big overgrown baby on your hands."

With the video evidence and Kris' prior record, the verdict was a forgone conclusion. Kris was promptly sentenced to 8 months in "juvie" after being found guilty of theft.

Judge Robinson called up Brett next. When the Judge

read his file, he asked Jackie, "Did you bring your sister with you?"

"Yes, sir."

Tasha stood up beside Jackie.

The judge looked at Tasha. "Were you in charge of Brett yesterday afternoon?"

Tasha replied in a low voice, "Yes, Your Honor."

"When it started to get dark, why weren't you out looking for him? Why didn't you call the police?"

"I knew he was somewhere in the neighborhood. I thought that maybe he just lost track of the time at the basketball court or something."

The judge assigned Brett Jr. a counselor, who would make unannounced home calls and stop by at any time. He told Tasha in a stern voice, "The court will expect you to know where he is at all times."

"Yes, Your Honor."

On the way home from court, Lisa shed a few tears as she was talking to Jackie. She told Jackie, "You know, try to keep up with Brett Jr. a little more. You don't want him locked up like Kris." Then she contradicted herself somewhat. "The counselor comes by for the first few weeks, then you don't have to see him again."

In a few days, Jackie really cleaned up her act. She got her phone back on and cleaned up the house. She wasn't doing the club scene too much lately either, going occasionally on the weekends. She didn't keep her promise about going to the drug treatment program and kept trying to convince her family that she could stop using drugs on her own, even though she was still getting high in the bathroom while the boys were upstairs asleep.

* * *

Brett Sr. got the word from off the street about what was going on with Jackie. He'd heard about her hanging out at all hours of the night, that Mrs. Smalls had taken Tammy because of her wild lifestyle, and that his eldest son went to jail. He knew that she was never home, and that the boys were practically raising themselves. He'd also heard that she never dressed them in decent clothes, and that they always had on cheap sneakers.

Brett Sr. told his boy James, "This is the perfect opportunity to take one of my sons." He figured this would be a good way to avoid paying any child support. In fact Brett often talked with his wife about wanting to spend more time with his eldest son, his namesake, to raise him the right way.

Brett saw Lisa, to sell her some drugs. After he hooked her up, he asked her for Jackie's phone number.

When Lisa gave it to him, he said to her, "Is it true that Jackie was at the bar getting high when Brett Jr. got in trouble?"

Lisa told him how his sons had been watching themselves on many occasions, and that when they were at home asleep, Jackie would slip out for a few hours and leave them home alone.

Brett later called Jackie. "I'm coming over to talk to you."

"Why? I'm not dropping the child support case!"

Brett said, "It's not about that. It's about the children."

When Brett arrived at the house, Brett Jr. was already outside, so Jackie told Benny to go out in front of the house for a little while.

Brett Sr. spoke in a reasonable tone to Jackie. "Brett Jr. is getting into trouble, and he is at the age where he really needs a man in his life. Why don't you let him come stay with me and Debbie? She has a son that is his age, a really good kid, an A and B student."

Jackie shook her head. "No, he doesn't even know you all."

"He will never get to know us if you don't give it a try."

Jackie thought about it for a while. Then she said, "I'm not too sure."

"I would hate to catch the boys home asleep by themselves, or bring the people from Children's Services to the bar where you hang out."

Then Brett started talking about taking the case to court, and about how he had a complete and stable family. He even told her that he knew that she was getting high, and about her sister lying to the court.

Seeing how scared Jackie looked, Brett softened. "Let's try it for a couple of months, and if it don't work out, you can take him back. Just think all you would be responsible for is Benny, because I heard Tammy stays with your mom now."

Jackie felt trapped, like she had no choice. "What about the money every month?"

Brett snapped, "I shouldn't have to pay you anything because *I* have one and *you* have one."

"Uh-uh. No deal. I took care of Brett Jr. for twelve years and Benny for ten, and you never gave me a dime."

Brett scratched his head. He thought he almost had her beat. "Okay. I will pay three hundred a month back pay and that's it!"

"Okay, we can give it a try. Let's explain it to the boys."

Jackie called the boys into the house and told them what was going on.

Brett Jr. didn't look too happy about it, but he didn't say anything outside of, "I'd give it a chance."

With Brett Jr. gone, Jackie decided she wasn't going to take any chances with leaving Benny home alone. She knew she had to go about things differently especially since her family was so disappointed that she didn't keep her promise about seeking help.

She thought about going to see Ann. Ann was the neighborhood babysitter, and all the children called her Auntie Ann. She had five children of her own and lived a short bus ride from Jackie's place.

She told Jackie, "On the days that you have something to do, I would watch Benny for you, but I can't promise to pick him up or drop him off. I have enough to do with my own."

Jackie nodded. "So how much you charge?"

"Fifteen dollars a day."

As soon as Jackie realized she had a steady baby-sitter, she got completely out of control. She began acting like she had no responsibilities at all. In fact, having just Benny made her worse than she already was since it was so easy for her to pay someone to watch him while she ran the streets.

She would take the bus, drop Benny off with a cold cut sandwich and a juice, and pick him up late at night, often with some guy or whoever would give her a ride home. Now Benny wasn't getting his proper sleep, hot meals, baths, or help with his homework.

When the court counselor who was supposed to come by periodically and check on Jackie and the boys never did so, the family knew something wasn't right. They wanted to call the courts themselves, but they didn't want to see the boys end up getting taken away from their mother.

On the other side of town, Brett Jr. was living a much safer and better life, something he wasn't used to it, and he hated it. Unlike with Jackie, there was no room for him to do whatever he wanted. First of all, he no longer walked to school, his step-mother drove him to school. Then as soon as he got home, he had to take a two-hour down-time to study and do his homework. After that he could go out and play basketball, baseball, or football, which could all be done right in front of the house. It felt weird to him because the whole neighborhood did everything, ate dinner, came outside after school, around the same time.

Brett Jr. didn't like being on a schedule. Everything revolved around his step-mom Debbie and step-brother Rob. He was always around them, and the only time he would see his dad was before he went to sleep and whenever he woke up.

One night, when they thought Brett Jr. and Rob were asleep, Debbie and Brett Sr. got into an argument.

Slips of conversation floated into Brett Jr.'s bedroom.

"I don't think you spend enough time with Brett Jr."

"You only brought him here so I would have to take care of him. I have enough responsibility to take care of Rob. This is your responsibility to take care of your own child."

Brett replied, "I only took him in because Jackie wasn't doing right and because she didn't deserve all of the money she was getting."

There was a lull in the argument.

Brett Sr. lowered his voice. "I don't think it's taking advantage of you, since you're taking Rob to school and picking him up anyway. What difference does one more child make?"

After Brett Jr. overheard their conversation, he felt like he wasn't wanted there, so he decided he was going to start getting in trouble so they would send him back to his mom's house.

Later that week, Rob and Brett Jr. were watching a TV show about a gunfight.

"We have the same type of gun," Rob said.

That gave Brett Jr. an idea. "Dad has a gun like that?"

"Yes, but he keeps it hid."

After a little bribing, Rob told Brett Jr. where Brett Sr. hid his gun.

When weekend came around and it was time for Brett Jr. to go see his mom, he slipped the gun that Rob had told him about under his jacket.

The following Friday evening around 7 p.m., Annette and Tasha were out doing some shopping, and in-between stores, they stopped at Popeye's to get a bite to eat. As they got in line they saw Benny sitting in the corner, eating a meal. They ordered their food to go then went over to talk with him.

Annette asked him, "How did you get here?"

"I caught the bus."

"And where is your mother?"

"I don't know."

Finally, he admitted to his aunts that Jackie had dropped him off at Aunt Ann's house and given him some money to get something to eat because she didn't have time to cook, and that she would pick him up later that evening.

Annette asked him, "Did the lady know that you caught the bus here?"

Benny shook his head. "I told her that I was walking to the neighborhood store. But when I got there I didn't feel like eating another cold cut sandwich so I decided to catch the bus to get something hot."

Between themselves, Tasha and Annette decided to take Benny to Annette's house. When she first saw him at the mall, Annette had already made up her mind that she was going to let him stay with her for a while. But first she decided to buy him a change of clothes and some new boots.

Once there, she got to her house, she gave him a nice hot bath.

Benny settled down and made himself at home. He just played Sony PlayStation until he fell asleep.

At 3 a.m. when Jackie finally went to Aunt Ann's house to pick Benny up, she was told that her son never came back from the store.

"I thought that he had run into you and that you'd just took him with you," Aunt Ann informed her.

At that point Jackie started to panic. She ran frantically out of the house and jumped into the car with some guy she had just met at the bar. She started yelling at the man, "Drive. Run through red lights if you have to."

It was a wonder they didn't kill themselves, or some-body else, trying to get to her mother's house. As soon as she got there, Jackie started yelling, "Where is Benny?

Where is he?" She ran through the house, checking all the rooms and waking everybody up, screaming, "Benny! Benny! Where are you?"

Tasha asked her, "What the hell are you talking about?"

Jackie started slobbering and crying. "I'm looking for Benny. Tasha, please tell me he's here."

Tasha looked at her blankly. "You don't know where your own child is? You should call the police."

"No! I can't call the police, and you already know what would happen." She threw her hands up in frustration and said, "I will find him myself," then ran out of the house.

Within a half-hour, she ran back to her mother's house. All she could do was lie on the floor and cry.

The family was hoping that somehow Jackie would get off the floor and realize that the longer she lay there the more time she was wasting. She was blowing every chance of finding her son.

Her mom couldn't take any more. Tears started to roll down her cheeks. She couldn't let Jackie suffer any longer. Mrs. Smalls knew that Jackie was hurting because she didn't know where Benny was, or if he was alive or dead, and she didn't want to involve the police and risk her losing her children.

Everyone in the family all felt the same way. They all decided that enough was enough. They were afraid themselves and didn't know where to draw the line. They were hoping Jackie would hang herself, and get scared straight, but their plan for intervention had backfired. When they set up the plan, they didn't make allowances for Jackie being able to pull at their heartstrings when she cried.

Finally, Jackie's mom sat on the floor beside her and put her head in her lap.

As Jackie lay there, whooping and hollering, her mom shushed her. Finally she told her, "Benny's all right, Jackie. Calm down." She added, "We can't keep covering for you. Baby, you need to get help for yourself. Please, Jackie, I love you, but you're going to have to get help before it's too late." Mrs. Smalls had never sounded more serious.

Even after her mom told her that Benny was all right, Jackie still kept crying. She really felt truly sorry for the first time.

Once she stopped crying, Jackie agreed to get help after her birthday, which was coming up in two weeks.

"I know I've been a mess," she said, "but I've never said I would go into a program before. I want to get help."

She decided to ask her new job at the health clinic to help her enter a program. That way she would still have her job and they'd still pay her while she was in the program.

Chapter 22

Across town . . .

A day later, Debbie took Rob and Brett Jr. along with her to run some errands. They ended up at a grocery store, where she stocked up on food for the house. As they were leaving, Debbie remembered that she had forgotten to get something. She wanted to send one of the boys in for it, but since they couldn't use her credit card, she decided to pick it up herself.

Standing in the checkout line, she saw customers running in the parking lot. "I wonder what's going on?" she mused out loud.

As she got to the door she saw Brett Jr. behind the driver's seat of her van as it crashed into the driver's door of a little old lady's car. Rob was in the passenger seat, riding shotgun.

Later, Brett Jr. told the police that he just wanted to take a joyride around the parking lot. Rob had tried to stop him at the last minute, but it was too late.

The old lady had to be taken to the hospital for minor injuries and was kept under observation. Debbie was also informed that the insurance company wasn't going to pay for the damages because a minor was driving during the time of the accident.

When Brett Sr. got the news, he called Jackie right away. The first words out of his mouth were, "I'm not paying you another dime of back pay. Now, I have to help pay for the damages that Brett Jr. did to Debbie's car."

Jackie told him, "Those damages have nothing to do with me and the money you already owed me on the back child support."

"I ain't paying you shit."

"Well then, if that's the way you want it, I'm taking your ass back to court."

Later that evening, Brett Sr. took Brett Jr. home. "We can't handle him anymore," he said, giving him back to Jackie.

All that night, Jackie paced the floor. She had so many things on her mind. She wondered who would take the children while she was in the program. Her life was reeling out of control, and she seemed powerless to do anything about it.

She also wondered what she was going to do for money. She'd found a new receptionist job at the health clinic, but it was only going to pay for so much. She needed to clear her mind from all that was troubling her. She thought of leaving the house, but Benny was due to come home tonight or tomorrow, and she knew she had to be around.

The next day after school, Annette brought Benny home.

Jackie then asked her mother, "Would you keep an eye out for the children for me? I want to take care of some business." She wanted to get high just one more time before entering the program.

Mrs. Smalls nodded. It appeared to the family that there had been a change in Jackie, that she'd finally learned her lesson. But when Jackie came back late that evening around 7:30 p.m. to pick up the children, Mrs. Smalls was worried.

By this time, the boys were already fed. All they needed was to take their baths.

"Is everything all right, Jackie?" Mrs. Smalls asked wearily. She'd noticed that Jackie was smelling of alcohol and looked as if she was high.

Jackie rushed the boys out the door and tried to reassure her mother. "Mom, everything is fine. Don't worry so much. I'll see you tomorrow."

After the boys took their baths, they went to bed. Jackie still had the urge to get a little higher, but she knew that she needed to be alert for the children.

When she couldn't fight the urge any longer, she picked up the phone and called a cab to take her to the club.

When she got there to buy her stuff, Lisa stopped her on her way out the door. "Hey, girl, I can give you a ride home. That way you won't have to pay for a cab. Why don't you stay for one more drink?"

Jackie was glad to stay out and continue enjoying herself. "Okay, but I can't stay long."

Once they started drinking some more, Jackie forgot all about the time.

In the meantime, Brett Jr. had gotten out of bed. When he realized that his mom wasn't at home, he decided to go out to see his friends.

Benny heard the door close. When he saw his older brother leave, he decided to follow him. Benny caught up with Brett and his friends at the corner.

"Go on back home, Benny. I'll be back. I just want to hang with my home boys."

Benny put up a fight. He threw such a fit that Brett was embarrassed in front of his boys.

Brett finally got Benny to go upstairs, following him back in the house to make sure that he didn't come back out.

Benny got so angry, he started throwing things around.

"Man, stop this, Benny, before I kick your ass."

Before Benny knew what happened, Brett knocked him down and socked him.

In a fit of anger, Benny ran to the closet and found the gun that Brett had taken from their father's house. He aimed it at Brett, mainly to scare him.

Brett tried to take it from him and a struggle ensued. During the struggle, the gun went off, and Brett was hit in the neck and slumped to the floor, blood gushing all over the bed, the floor, and the spreads.

In disbelief, Benny dropped the gun, darted down the stairs, straight out of the door, and headed towards his grandmother's house. When he got to her door, he banged and banged.

It was twelve at night. He woke Mrs. Smalls up and

scared everyone in the house. The lights went on in the living room.

Tasha answered the door. "Benny, what's the matter?"

Benny was crying and yelling, "I killed him. I didn't mean it. I killed him!"

Tasha and the family kept asking Benny, "Who? What are you talking about?"

But Benny appeared to be in shock, and he was too hysterical to make sense. "I killed him," he said over and over.

Finally Tasha and Yolanda ran over to Jackie's house and arrived at the same time as the police. The neighbor next door had called 9-1-1 after she'd heard a gunshot. By then everyone in the projects had their heads out the window or were outside in front of Jackie's house.

The police entered first, their guns drawn, because they didn't know if there was an assailant still on the premises. When they got upstairs, they found Brett Jr. in his room's doorway, lying in a pool of blood. They called the ambulance and checked the rest of the house, then told Tasha to come identify the kid that had been shot.

Chapter 23

Distraught as she was, Tasha cooperated with law enforcement. She told the police that the victim was indeed her nephew. "His brother is over my house crying. He accidentally shot his brother. He didn't mean to hurt him."

One of the policemen asked, "So who was watching them?"

This time Tasha told the truth. "My sister, their mother, often leaves them home alone. I hate to say it, but she's strung out on that crack."

The police nodded his head.

Tasha told them the places that Jackie hung out at, where they could probably find her.

Subsequently, the police put a warrant out for Jackie's arrest then went next door and took Benny down to Juvenile Detention and questioned him.

"Don't worry, Brett," Tasha said, holding his hand. "I'm here."

Brett was semi-unconscious, coming in and out, and Tasha rode with him to the hospital.

Annette picked up Mrs. Smalls and met Tasha at the hospital.

Later, Jackie was picked up at the bar and told the news by the officers.

Two officers, one white and the other black, also went to Brett Sr.'s house.

Debbie answered the door.

The police asked her, "Do you have a gun in the house?"

Debbie's eyes grew wide with fear. "My husband has one downstairs."

"Could you show us . . . because Brett Jr. was shot by his brother, who told us it was Brett Sr.'s gun and this is where he's been staying."

Debbie escorted the police downstairs to the family room. The gun was gone from where Brett had always kept it.

The police asked her, "Do y'all have a permit?"

She said, "No."

One of the officers said, "Tell Brett Sr. to come to the station and turn himself in because we will be issuing a warrant for his arrest."

With that, both officers left the home.

Brett later went down to the station and was able to get out on bond. Thereafter, he was only given probation since he had no criminal record.

Later on that night, Jackie was allowed to make a phone

call. She called her mother's house. "I just want to know if Brett Jr. survived?"

Natasha sounded cold. "He's going to make it, Jackie, but he is paralyzed from his neck down for life." She slammed the phone down.

For the longest time, Jackie stood there, holding the phone, shocked.

The situation shook up the entire Smalls family. They had been through a lot together, but this was a case of enabling. Now they felt that because they didn't crack down on Jackie sooner, she never got to hit rock bottom. Because she never suffered the consequences of her actions, she never had a reason to change or seek help, the very thing the Smalls family was trying to avoid. Jackie didn't only lose her boys, she lost her freedom.

The family felt they were to blame because they could have turned Jackie in, but didn't. In trying to stick together as a family and be there for her, they had indirectly aided and abetted her drug problem. Now, Brett Jr.'s life was destroyed, and it even looked like it was too late to help Jackie.

And Tasha's life would never be the same. Her lie would come back to haunt her whenever she saw her nephew, Brett Jr., trying to maneuver in a wheelchair.

Yet, in spite of how Jackie's life had impinged upon hers, Tasha still had to show support for her sister when she went to court for sentencing. After all, she was family.

Chapter 24

A year later . . .

Tamika walked out of the women's prison after a visit with her mother and heaved a deep sigh. It was like this every time. She always felt more depressed than uplifted after visiting her mother. Jackie and Tamika had cried throughout the whole visit.

At first she used to visit Jackie in prison with her Auntie Tasha, or her other aunts and her grandmother, but everyone's schedule had gotten so busy. Her grandmother was busy taking Brett to physical rehabilitation therapy. Mrs. Smalls still had hope that Brett, Jr. would one day be able to walk again.

Now that it was summer, Tamika had started catching the bus out to the prison alone. After all, she was seventeen. And as poor of an excuse for a mother that Jackie had been, she was still her daughter.

"Baby, I'm so sorry," Jackie said over and over.

Tamika was glad when the hour-visit was over. Stepping outside, she looked up at the sun then shielded her eyes. She felt so old for seventeen. She didn't like seeing Jackie locked up, but she had gotten tired of waiting for the other shoe to drop. She'd known since she was about nine years old that their family life was not normal, that Jackie was headed for a fall.

From the time she was nine, Tamika had to grocery shop, cook dinner, and put her brothers to bed. It was as though an epidemic had hit the whole neighborhood and just about everyone's mother she knew was getting high. But as long as she had her grandmother, she didn't worry. She knew her grandmother would take them in, and eventually, she did take full custody of Tamika, her brothers going to their father.

Sometimes Tamika wondered about her father. She knew now that Roger had been like an adoptive father. Through the grapevine, she'd heard a guy named Kenny, one of Jackie's high school boyfriends, was her biological father, but who cared? Whoever this Kenny was had never sought out a relationship with her and she didn't want to have one with him.

The only problem was that her grandmother and aunts watched her so closely. She was still a virgin, and she had no plans of changing that, but she would've liked to go to some parties and loosen up a bit sometimes.

"I'll never be like Jackie," Tamika vowed to herself. She knew things were bad, but she'd never dreamed her brother Brett would end up in a wheelchair and her mother behind bars.

She often looked at her baby pictures where she was

wrapped in her mother's and stepfather's arms. They had looked so happy together.

Now and then, when Jackie was high, she had told Tamika that Roger was the only man that had truly loved her. Tamika wished she could remember Roger, but she had been too young. She remembered Brett, her brothers' father, but those weren't good memories for her, as he often made her mother cry.

While other girls were worrying about prom and who their date would be, Tamika was wondering if her life would ever be normal. Lost in thought, she adjusted her backpack and trudged to the bus stop. Her camisole felt damp with sweat and clung to her back. Her thighs swished against her jeans as she walked. She wiped her forehead.

Usually, there were other people standing at the stop, but today the stop was deserted, and she knew she'd have to wait at least an hour for the next bus, since the prison was outside of the city limits. Although the bus supposedly ran every hour, the last time Tamika visited, two weeks earlier, she had to wait for three hours.

A voice pierced her thoughts. "Hey, good-lookin'."

Tamika looked up to see a muscular young guy riding a motorcycle. He was wearing shades and a sleeveless leather jacket and tight pants. He was built, what the high school girls called "buff," and he had a large tattoo emblazoned on his upper bicep with the name "Rock."

"Do I know you?" Tamika asked cautiously.

"No, baby. My name is Rock. What's yours?"

"Why?"

"I just want to offer you a ride back to the city."

"I don't know."

"It's a long wait for the bus. You sure?"

Tamika thought about the last time she had waited three hours for the bus. She weighed it. Should she or shouldn't she take his ride? She'd never ridden on a motorcycle before. She felt excited at the thought. After all, she was seventeen. She was a big girl. She could handle herself.

Rock smiled encouragingly, a gold tooth flashing in the blinding sun. "C'mon, you'll be all right."

Tamika looked around as if expecting to see her grandmother. Then she remembered her grandmother and her watchful aunts were all in the city. She'd always been a good girl. Maybe it was time to take a few chances and live a little. She didn't have to turn out like Jackie. "Okay." She climbed on the back of the motorcycle, wrapped her arms around Rock's firm waist, grimacing as he sped off from the curb in a blaze of smoke.